THE DEATH
OF
THE WAVE

THE DEATH
OF
THE WAVE

G. L. Adamson

Greyhart Press

www.greyhartpress.com

Beta Reader Team

The author and publisher wish to thank our beta reader team for *The Death of the Wave*. We had invaluable comments and suggestions from:

David Ferretti
Duck Grossberg
Misha Herwin
Jaymie Krambeck
Nicholas Matherne
Sally Ontiveros
Dave Pollock
Michael Sterlacci
Christopher Szutenbach

Thank you, all!

If you're interested in joining our beta reader teams, drop us a line at editors@greyhartpress.com or tweet @GreyhartPress

This work is dedicated to my supportive friends and family. A special thanks to the 'Bat-cave': Chris, Jaymie, V, and Mike, who have stuck with me through the entire writing and editing process. To my mother for her patience and keen eye, to my professors who have encouraged me, and to the KCACTF crew for making me a better writer than I ever could have thought possible. Sebastian, Annie, and Nick especially, this is for you. A big thank you to Bridget for her excitement about my work and all the writers I am currently working with online. To all the master writers who have inspired me my entire life, and another thanks to my publisher Tim Taylor for being fantastic throughout this entire process. Thank you, thank you, thank you.

A story spanning over sixty years. Time is fluid, running from the present, to memory, and back again, to form a tale taken from the minds of three protagonists.

SECTIONS

The State of Eden.

A world that was once our world. A State where standardized testing and the Citizen Evaluation Exam governs the lives of the masses, and there is sharp delineation between those who are gifted in science and mathematics and the rest of the populace, between Camps and Palaces, between rich and poor. Welcome to a world where genetically engineered humans compete with all others in a quest for intellectual dominance. Welcome to a State where a single reminder of the past can get you killed.

Welcome to the rule of law without morality that shudders upon the brink of revolution.

Welcome to Eden.

THE MAJOR PLAYERS

BREAKER 256
The Martyr

A policewoman of the State, or Breaker, who begins the revolution against the State.

A writer who is hired to go against the revolution who sees his beliefs challenged.

BLUE
The Artist

COMET
Child 56409
The Scientist

A young man who is hired to work as a scientist for the State.

A genetically engineered human who is the leader of the State.

GALILEO
Human Services Coordinator
The King

NEWTON
Human Services Assistant
The Voice of Eden
The Lord

A genetically engineered human who is second-in-command of the State.

A genetically engineered human who aids in the revolution. Son of GALILEO.

DESCARTES
The Aristo Who Wrote

DARWIN
The Prince.

A human genetically engineered in a way unforeseen. Son of GALILEO.

Eden's head policeman/Breaker, a contemporary of BREAKER 256.

BREAKER 376
The Warden

AUTHOR

The savior of the Camps, known only through writing. Several anonymous individuals.

PROLOGUE

Ex igne veritas

This world
ever was,
and is,
and shall be,
ever-living fire,
in measures being kindled
and
in measure going out.
—*Heraclitus*

15

INCIPIENT

BLUE

Whose son am I?
I close my eyes in the waiting and thank myself for a hiding
place.
The precious things of broken men.
A notched stick,
a scrap of letter,
paper.
I can see my kingdom traced behind my eyelids as if fired
behind by the sun.
Cot. Sink. Toilet. Wall.
Sometimes I see fantastic images in the stone,
and other times I see nothing.
Yesterday there were tigers with outstretched claws,
as if come back from the dead.
I have never seen a tiger outside of one picture, though there
were mentions of an elderly male,
the last of his kind,
still languishing in a zoo somewhere beyond the Hives when I
was a child.
No tigers today.
There exists nothing else but to wait for the five strikes
of the heavy iron tongue in the clock tower.

Soon there will be bread.

The ring of the clock-tower in the Citadel, for the new voice will sound over Eden.

The old voice and his lord are dead.

Long live the king.

Edict 10975, the rights of the Breakers.

A cough from the man across from me, dry and desperate.

Soon there will be nothing left.

For I, myself, am alone and

I smile, knowing the mechanics to be easy.

It is best to think, best to remember, or to risk forgetting.

When we were first brought into the Barracks, we still strutted as if we were soldiers, and murmured all sacrifices' names loosely behind cupped hands.

Now we only wait, and eat the bread of dead men.

No, I will remember the lies.

I will remember my name.

PART ONE: DORMANT

EDICT 4907: The Citizen Evaluation Exam is fair. It does not discriminate against race, class, or creed. If a man revolts against his just position and place in life, that man will be imprisoned or else put to death.

The war never ends. Only the enemies change.

BREAKER 256

I waited, for once at peace within the Artists' slums
and listened as the clock-tower in the Citadel, far off, far off,
rang six.
For another hour, Newton, the Voice of Eden, blared out over
the sound-waves,
today: the Censor's listing, the banning of the books,
and the Citadel controls all allotment and use of technology.
A young couple strolled idly by in the gloom.
I could tell that they were young by the ease with which they
strolled,
they had not yet learned to fear the night, as they should have.
But this was their kingdom, and they strutted like the king and
queen of beggars.
The youth looked straight at me and his eyes blazed with a secret
threat.
I only smiled and adjusted, revealing the stunner gun strapped
to my hip.
He knew that I could drag him to the Barracks, under the care
of Lady Justice
and looked away, his arm too tight around his girl.

I was, I am recognized.
Enemy.
Breaker.

I kept the balance in the slums and in the palaces of the elite.
My presence was reminiscent of the sweaty Hives where the
orphans are kept
and of the hellish Barracks and the Factories where citizens are
detained.
I am everything and nothing.
I was
I am
neutral.
But there, I affected the easy stance of a poet beyond caring.
My badge was contained neatly in my coat pocket,
256
and Eden's oak tree insignia was carefully covered by my coat.
For Poet's Camp.
For the benefit of the Artists.
I knew their leader, Dante, dead these months, and they
tolerated me.
When I was with them, I was home.
For the sudden fires in the shanty-town beckoned me and
the musicians had made their peace with the poets.
So faint, so faint, a fiddle sounded as if gathering up all the
sadness in the world.
There, in the poorest edge of the ghetto.
It was always alive with the buzzing of words, the blending
together of a thousand images.
A woman sung her baby to sleep with a snippet of poetry set to
the lonely music.
I wondered if the words had meaning for her, or if they were
just nonsense, a part of a history long denied, as beautiful as they
were empty.
I hummed along quietly under my breath and earned a startled
glance.

Calmly, I walked over to the fire.

The huddle made room for me, and wordlessly,

I was given a piece of their meat by a man who would not meet
my eyes.

The fiddle music swooped and I watched the motley group
as they remained silent for my benefit.

The night, it still suffers from the bright flares over the Camps.

They write no poems about stars, nor dare to lift their heads.

But one began to murmur a bit of Shakespeare as the fiddler
slowed his bow,

his deep sonorous tones achingly familiar.

I thought that his name was Sonnet and his face was familiar as
well, neither old nor young,

but he gathered the ragged children as if they were his own.

He intoned about tomorrow and the great betrayal of Scottish
kings.

How melancholy and how beautiful!

But what of Scotland, and what is Scotland?

Tomorrow.

A desolate word, under dying skies, dropped like a coin down a
well.

Out, out brief candle.

I trembled, and one of their skinny mongrels lifted his head and
bayed at the sickle moon.

Roasting meat.

Bright fire.

Molasses words under a too-bright sky.

BLUE

I'm not sure how I got involved in all of this.
Certainly my beginning was unremarkable.
I was born in an Artist Camp somewhere, I was assured, and
sold or given into the Hive system.
It was assumed that I was born into the largest Writer's Camp,
where most of the orphans had been coming from.
Lack of food and even poorer water supplies had driven the poor
bastards out,
and in the North, under leader Tolkien, the population boom
had been too much for them.
People were starving,
but compared to my potential fate, the Hives weren't all that
bad.
Mine was shabby but well-cared for, and the Head Keeper was
distant but affable.
The kids slept in iron-runged bunks during the night, fifty to a
dormitory,
and in the morning trudged off to whatever rooms could be
spared to prepare for the tests.
Testing prep began at age six, half way to the Citizen Evaluation
Exams,
and these mock exams served as a kind of training ground for
the real thing.
They also served a far more important purpose, as the kids who
failed the mocks could be
Marked.
Winnowed
out from the intense prep and save the teacher Keepers their
valuable time.

The lesson was clear—fail a mock and you would fall behind,
and failing the CEE could be fatal.

Citizen Evaluation Exam.

Everyone took it the year of their twelfth birthday
and your entire life had been leading up to this moment.

It was a lottery roll based on pure brain-power.

Score high on the science and mathematics sections, and your
life was pretty much assured. You'd be sent to the Palaces to
dwell in the world of the aristos, working in their labs,
building their bridges, calculating their busy-work.

Score high on reading comprehension and analysis, and you
were off to the Camps, your talents geared towards usefulness in
the world of the Censor.

Score low on all sections, and you had but a small prayer of
surviving.

Intellect is the currency in our delightful society.

The race is no longer to the swift, nor the jerk to the strong and
fools are not suffered to live.

It is a simple question of resources.

This is the way it has always been.

Who marks that it can change, or even if it should?

One life. One test.

The kids in the Hives against the kids in the ghettos.

The kids in the ghettos against the kids in the Palaces.

The norm kids in the Palaces against the aristos, genetic
engineering.

Brilliance bred.

An uneven gamble.

One life, one test.

COMET

I was child 56409.
My age set was Youth.
My Hive number, 45834.
There was nervousness in the holding area where our cots were.
Some of the other boys were scared and they worked slowly
through their Citizen Evaluation Exam workbooks.
The workbooks were dog-eared, some had pages missing, some
were water-logged.
Mine was singed as if the kid that had it before me had let his
lamp burn low.
The clock tower rang out seven and the edict remained.
Edict 90865, the fate of a thief.
I put my book to the side, and I stared at the ceiling, all around
me hearing
the whispered scratches of graphite and paper.
7897 was breezing through his at a thousand miles per minute.
He was sure to pass.
I told him to score high.
But he did not answer.
The pencil they gave me had perfect teeth marks.

BREAKER 256

I felt like I am one of them.
I am like them.
It was so warm and so quiet.
A young woman carefully stroked my arm to feel the fabric of
my coat.
She whispered a name that sounded like Poesy.
Names in the Artist slums mean everything.
They indicate tribe and offshoot profession and status in the
tribe.
In all things specificity counts.
She asked me mine and there I hesitated.
None of us start out with names; it is when we are tested into
our lives
that we take our names and our place in society.
Because Breakers never chose which side, Breakers are nameless.
We only gain a different life-number.
But I could not give them my number, as they would know then
of my profession.
I told her that my name is Byron.
She did not get the reference.
I relaxed slightly and thought of how these names were just
names, without any history.
They were only words in a void, repeated for so long that they
had been leached of all meaning.
I was born in the Camps.
I was not always a Breaker, a killer of my own people, a cog in
the machine.
I grew up in a place like this, in one of the Writer's Camps in
the bowels of Eden.

I knew all about being hungry, testing in the mock tests in the
Hives and ducking the recruiters.
I had seen men with dirty faces, and I was a Camps child in the
street
before they put a weapon in my hands and a lie in my heart.
What choice did I have when the results came back to stare me
in the face?
A tiny chance, an equal score, the Palaces or the slums and their
tiny warring factions—
If I became a Breaker, there would be bread for my mother and
little brother. We would be taken from the Camps and placed
outside the Barracks with the other Breakers.
I would be given authority, my face wiped clean, a uniform,
bread—
My little brother would have his fate decided when he took his
CEE,
but my mother was safe, provided for.
I made the right decision
and so have no regret.
I cannot regret.
My eyes slowly closed, Sonnet's droning echoing in my mind.
I was the enemy, and these people distrusted me.
But I am, I must be
like you.
There was, is, something in me that reminded them of an aristo,
and inspired instinctive dread—those pale gaunt synthetic
beauties.
Genetically engineered humans bred for beauty and mind and—
cruelty.
But I am not.
I am but their guard dog.
I was Breaker, but the fire was warm and I was near asleep.

It was only the low warning hum of a stunner gun that broke
my trance.
I nearly missed the tall Breaker in the shadows, clothed in sleek
black and watching me.
I studied him curiously with sinking apprehension.
He was not attempting to blend into Poet's Camp.
My pitiful disguise, interrupted by a Bohemian scarf like a
distress flag, did not throw him off.
My identity.
I remembered that smooth death's head.
376.
Strange to see him back from the Hives.
He is defined by me, the shadow a solid figure casts.
He waited and he watched, his stunner prepped, and I knew
that he would have informed
the Palaces without hesitation if I was lenient.
For he had nothing left to lose.
Sonnet said it best, that one may smile and smile, and yet still be
a villain.
But all things and all smiles would stop altogether.
So I killed the man whose words were music.
I killed him in front of the fire.

COMET

Did you hear?
Horror stories in the midst of the season, the night before the
CEE.
56859 told me of the outcomes of the last CEE.
He slept in the bunk across from mine.
Did I hear of the boy who got into the Palaces and found out he
had family back in the Camps?
Did I hear that he threw his future away?
A few boys and a girl failed the test last time in our Hive and
were taken in
for a retest for the entire district.
The scores of the failures were compared not by the Keepers, but
a Breaker.
Governmental business.
Did I hear who survived?
A girl, a lower number than us, her family from the Perform
Camps, she got the highest score.
The others were killed.
I pictured them in my mind, even though 56859 assured me
they were taken outside,
that it was humane.
That the Keepers, the Breakers lie, that it is not spoken of—
I pictured a Breaker in his black uniform, setting his gun on the
students at their desks.
But what of the girl that lived?
She was sent to below the poverty line, 56859 told me, to
scrounge along the edges of society.
Her idiocy tattooed in bright ink.

BREAKER 256

I never knew shame to have a taste, but it tasted like metal as
I climbed the stairs of the capital Citadel.
My scarf had been discarded and my clothing stank of blood,
but the steps shone like pure marble.
I stumbled near the top and a hand grabbed mine,
blunt like wood, with dried blood under the fingernails.
Once before had he offered his hand to me when I had fallen,
but this time I did not pull away.
Breaker 376 nodded to me and helped me to my feet.
His head is narrow like a whippet dog and there is strength and
serenity in his movements.
I did not like 376, but I respect him.
He is as honorable as a Breaker
as a traitor, could be,
and I saw why he had caught me.
An aristo stood in the sunlight.
He was tall, unnaturally tall and thin, even for an aristo, his
thigh the width of 376's arm.
The head was narrow and clever with a mouth like a slash in
parchment.
All this might have passed for human but his hands.
His hands, stretched palms, with their long, delicate fingers were
folded,
I was not to be touched with those peace-maker's hands.
Newton.
The Voice of Eden and Human Services Assistant, back from
the clock-tower.
The Voice of the State brushed my shoulder and those hands
were cold as the marble.

They gave me a medal for killing one of my own.
I never knew that they watched me, that they attempted to win me by
this *futile* gesture.
He put a gold medal around my neck,
held up by a ribbon as blue as a primordial sea.
He proclaimed my innocence and he raised my pay.
Two instances more and my little brother would have gotten
extra time on the CEE.
But why? Sonnet was not leader and Dante was dead.
Was it a diversion? A bribe?
To kill one of the last who remembered?
My soul was damned instead of ransomed,
For gold is worth much more than silver.
And as Newton touched my shoulder once more
I could see a streak of Sonnet's blood dried to a powder dart
across that cool white palm
and I trembled at the hang-man's hands.

BLUE

I stand outside in the curving line and resolutely search for the
sun.
There are so many of us, stamping our feet against the cold.
What are these men? These faces?
They are different, but all share that look of quiet desperation.
We are packed so tightly our window of sky is between the
heads of other men.
The Sickness
the Cull
has started.
The man in front of me is close.
His hair is falling out, and his eyes are shiny and blank.
He does not move,
and his shadow is weak on the snow.
What month, what year is it?
The air tastes of December and I hug myself in the cold like the
other men and feel my bones.
A shout hovers on the air.
A skeletal man, his eyes blazing canned fire is pulled by Breakers
and marched from the line.
The Cleaners in their pristine white uniforms and masks chatter
in swift high voices.
They wait for the order to inspect from the black limousine

that pulls up to the Barracks every Cleaning, the Palace car with
its tinted windows.
We have never looked inside.
What then, for the bartering of a life? An extra ration?
A plan drawn hastily with stick and ashes?
The man in front of me passes something down the line and
presses it listlessly into my hand.
Words. Words. Words.
What is considered precious about words?
What power do they hold, to blaze white-hot trails across mind
and soul?
If preciousness is considered in terms of rarity then what lunacy
is it to treasure words?
Spewed in their thousands, by infants, knaves and
madmen…what gamble is a life,
to clutch these words to my heart?
The order must have been given.
Cleaners move down the line, their strange bird-like masks with
empty eyes swaying
with their leisured gait,
their sticks prodding and questioning.
Every so often, the sticks will gesture, and another Breaker will
appear and lead
another dying man from the line.
At long last, the Cleaners have reached the end of the line and
stand in quizzical silence
as the shots begin to ring out,
the characteristic pow of an old-fashioned hand-gun,
the finishing buzz of a stunner.
We wait patiently, shivering in the cold.
One, two, three shots.
Three more rations of bread.

With thoughts of the food in our heads we enter our separate
kingdoms.
There is bread for us.
We eat in silence.
The old woman has cleaned my cell while the Cleaners cleaned
the hearts of men,
the woman with the face that is covered and the tall back that is
bent like a bow.
The letter burns with its metal clip close to my heart,
and I remember eyes like canned fire.
The aristo was killed in his cell by another prisoner.
One more shot and one more dead, one more dead, that means
more bread.
I smile to stave off forgetting.

PART ONE: DORMANT (Cont.)

COMET

The night before the test seemed to last forever, the morning
even longer.
I stood in the line with the other kids from the Hive.
56859 was in front of me and his face was white,
but as he saw me he winked as if he had a secret.
We sat in the cafeteria, amidst the hot steam and clatter of a
thousand dishes.
An hour until exams.
The Head Keeper, the one who told the stories of Author, he
smiled at us,
but the smile did not reach his eyes.
Breaker 376, with the narrow face and broad shoulders waited
by the door to discourage escape.
He held a rifle in his hands but as we passed he met my eyes,
and his gaze was dark and steady.
We lined up to go back to our bunks and change in the hurried
dark.
As I went to join the others who were ready for testing, 56859
ran up to me and pushed
a wrapped something into my hands.

"In case", he said, and I looked at him, a small dark figure
scrubbed almost crimson,
his uniform mended with bright blue patches.
I told him he was clever, and that he was not to worry.
He told me I was silly, and ran off to join the line.

BREAKER 256

The medal jangled upon my chest as I made my way towards the
Camps.
I stopped it with my hand.
My uniform had been cleaned and darned,
Sonnet's blood had long been washed away and
the insignia shined, no longer hidden for a Poet's benefit.
I glanced furtively around the corner, hoping not to spy a
Watchman.
They are under the Breakers, they go where it is far too
dangerous for Breakers to go.
Young and inexperienced, every Breaker pays their due as a
Watchman.
Although they are young, they are full of adolescent zeal,
and their warning red uniforms are that hue for a reason.
Blood-proof and highly visible.
I saw one wandering aimlessly down the street in alarming red
vinyl,
his dark hair gleaming under the street-lamps.
He was headed in the direction of the Perform Camps, and his
thin face
in the washed-out moonlight was young, and had the frailty of a
child.
I waited until I was certain I was out of his sight.
When I was certain, I removed the heavy medal and held it at
arm's length
and watched as it swayed and glinted insolently in my grip,
the bright copper tree of knowledge outstretching in all
directions
and the delicate insignia gleaming over its graceful branches:

Knowledge of the Edicts Will Set You Free.
I put it away, folding it into my pocket, and
entered into Writer territory and the Poet's outcropping.
An all-night pharmacy blinked bewilderedly into the night
with a line of stragglers still outside its dark doors.
It must have been the first of the month again, Citizens' health
care for free on the first.
Nutrition is poor for everyone here in Eden, especially in the
Camps,
and supplementary Proto-pills are meant to address this
problem.
The aristos told us that it was fair, but the life expectancy
discrepancy
still exists between the Camps and the Palaces.
Some of the aristos seem to live forever.

I turned to the entrance of Poet's Camp, when a dark mass
blocked my way.
It was 376.
The big man looked uneasy.
His dark eyes were fixed firmly on mine, but his hands were
twisting and untwisting, reaching for his gun and then relaxing
away.
His voice, ever familiar, was soft in the darkness.
"What are you doing here, 256?" he questioned levelly, direct and
serious.
"I am only doing my duty, 376," I responded calmly.
"Why are you out of the Hives? Did Galileo tell you to watch
over me?"
"That is irrelevant. Your shift is over."
I raised my head.
He looked away.

"You should go," I responded slowly,
and watched his implacable face,
the face that could not tell a lie,
as a tremor went through his frame.
He gazed at me again with troubled eyes.
"Go now," I urged quietly. "I will not be followed—"
He fretted and whispered: *"I will not be forced."*
Something had shattered in the great man's conscience,
and he shook his narrow head.
*"You are not wearing your medal. I knew of your hesitation. You
are sympathetic to the Camps—"*
"As I should be," I retorted, "we are from the Camps. Leave
now, 376."
He reached out for an instant, and rested his hand upon my
shoulder—
the banality of evil but we still had trained together.
"If I know anything about any intention contrary to the State," he
whispered,
"I will report it. I will not save you. I will do what must be done."
And with that, he turned, and left me to my work.

Poet's Camp was quiet, they must have been still mourning
Sonnet.
So.
Who was I, through their eyes?
Now that I am nothing?
What is it to be a Breaker?
It is to police the boundaries between Camps and Palaces,
to administer the remake tests,
to guard the jails.
*To be the guard dog of what passes for justice,
more the guardian of the aristocracy.*

41

Their eyes focused accusingly on my uniform,
on the revealed insignia that had been covered before.

I took the medal from my pocket
and placed it at a girl-child's feet and said:

"For you."

I was, I am, not one of them.

FLASH

BLUE

The aristo that was killed is not a major figure in my memories,
but he is there with me in my thoughts of the Barracks.
Aristos, they are hard to miss.
He towered over the other men, and his strange elongated face
had a self-absorbed look.
I never really gave him much thought.
Like all aristos he was elegant and imperious.
The striped Barrack uniform draped easily over his clothes-
hanger frame
with a grace that was alien to us.
He was only notable in that he was the first aristo most of us saw
up close.
Not me, however. I have seen enough aristos to last a lifetime.
I vaguely remember many of the other prisoners jostling him
like children at the zoo, wanting to look at those strange eyes
with their flat opal shine and to touch his freezing flesh.
He submitted placidly enough, but that thin mouth was closed
and trembling
with an inexpressible sadness, like a beast that would not speak if
it could.
Wait.
I search my memories.

Certainly that can't be right.
They have sadness bred out of them from birth, along with the
fullest extent of any emotion.
Aristos believed that emotions clogged the thinking.
But that downturned head, that flat dead gaze catching the light.
Sadness.

Say what you like, aristos are not like us.

Hatred, of course, existed for that poor skinny bastard, the
hungry men who looked past
how wretchedly thin he was and saw instead
a test weighted towards the Palaces,
the ringing out of the edicts every hour from the clock-tower,
a television with only three channels.
He hadn't long to live, we all knew that,
and we waited for the gunshot that would signal another ration.
We were beyond sadness for any man's death, certainly beyond
that of
a weird little aristo who never spoke.

When that last shot rang out, the prisoner with the fiery eyes
was already dead and gone.
We never questioned his wildness.
People broke all the time in the Barracks.
It was, you could say, the purpose of the place.
But still, I clutch the madman's letter to my heart,
meaning with the entirety of my being to later read it.
I unclip the piece of metal curved to keep it, and I save it.
The letter itself is written on the back of a booklet of Edicts,
a page torn out and given far away.
Edict 3462: The Choice of the Camps.

I read it as I eat my bread, the ink is dry and flaking.
The words straggle on as if they had to be chewed thoroughly
before being spat back out on the page.
This is the letter of a man who has to think carefully about every
syllable.

It's him.
Descartes.

Yes, I remember him now.
How different he was in the Palaces!
And all for the love of an Author.

I can see him in my mind, bent over the desk,
his glossy black hair obscuring those odd opal-eyes.
His hands move like magic and there is arithmetic in his fingers.
So there *was* still sanity in his head.
He pauses in his writing to hollow out another piece of the straw
that the Breakers leave us in the winter.
Another pause to his wrist and then he writes in his own ink,
like me,
with all my little tricks.

So it was not about the fiery-eyed outcast?
Almost a disappointment.

DESCARTES

My dearest reader:
If you are reading this, poor fool, you are in here with me.
I don't know why I have bothered to compose this letter, as your
chances of survival are also rather slim, but as it remains you are my
only hope.
How depressing.
But I have lived long enough.
Sometimes it feels as if I have lived forever.
My mind stalls and slows compared to the strange black-eyed
children
that can measure up to the machines.
These aristos, as you call them…they are somehow new.
I am not, I am only a step above the norms.
A mistake, or a test.
I remember the first sight that I saw
being the cool eyes of my father and his skin as white as marble.
Useless, really, but time goes slowly here, it stretches and it strains to
fill the hours of the day.
One must fill it up with something.
In my mind alone, here exists the memories of growing up in the
Palaces.
Aristocracy.
Private tutoring for the CEE which we are assured we would pass.

Fencing lessons to keep both mind and body sharp, the subtle contests against the Breakers.
My mother used to hold me against her skeletal chest and chant tunelessly a song of the periodic tables.

Boring, of course, to someone like you.

I wasn't like the others.
I wanted to learn everything, and was frustrated by the knowledge that was kept from me.
My father would watch me through slitted eyes over the dinner table as if that frustration was printed cleanly on my forehead.
I became more and less than the others:

The aristocrat who writes.

You may ask the purpose of this tirade.
I think that someone here in the Barracks is going to kill me.
They tolerated me at first, but their suspicions have overrun my novelty.
I intend, before the inevitable occurs, to tell someone of what I have seen and what I know.
I do not know if this will have an effect save to drive this letter into the hands of another,
or if you, dear reader, can even be trusted with this information.
But I am a dead man and so, most likely, are you.
Pity.
Wait until Cleaning day.
Hold the line.
I'll have him leave you a message.
Poor little fool, I wonder if you even remember what the world looks like outside the Barracks.

What else is there to do, but murmur your grievances
over and over to yourself in the face of an artificial night?
I wonder, if they blind you—will that make you sing?
One's sympathies are always on the side of life so-
Good luck, my poor fool, and fly for the both of us.

—*Descartes*

COMET

56859 said it wasn't always like this.
That there had been a time before the CEEs.
His mother who told him what it had been like before the
Censor,
had heard it long passed down the family line.
He was not like the other kids, he had a family back in Poet's
Camp,
but the Keeper said they sold him to pay for food years ago.
He thought that they would come back for him.
Every night he read a small booklet that he said
he smuggled in past the Breakers when he was delivered.
His mother gave it to him and it contains in tiny print all of
Eden's edicts.
It was supposed to keep him out of trouble.
It was supposed to keep him safe.
56859 was smart.
He said that he had been practicing poetry for when he got out
of the Hive,
but most of his work would never be written.

Ten minutes then, until they gave out the CEEs.
I was watching the Breaker in the corner of the classroom, but
56859 was looking at me.

I hid the booklet he gave me and I smiled to tell him his secret was safe.

He did not smile back.

BREAKER 256

Do I remember the genesis of my destiny?
That is easy.
It was after testing day, after the frantic ceremony, and the great
division of lives.
It is rather funny in retrospect, all the emphasis we place on the
CEE,
I hardly remember the test-taking process itself.
Stronger in my mind is my memory of the surrounding
circumstances, the trappings.
Number 2397, an unusually lanky boy chewing nervously on his
pencil, comes to mind,
as does number 2576, who played with her long flaxen hair as
she searched for the perfect word
for her essay on Sustainable Agriculture.
I admit that I glanced slightly at her work, something not worth
my life.
We, the adults, now build the exam up to be almost monolithic,
taking on a life of its own,
but it wasn't that horrible, truly.
I had my mother and my brother there to comfort me
before we were herded to the nearest Testing Center located in
the nearest Hive.
Testing day, we were fed better than usual in the Hive's shabby
cafeteria,
and those that still had mothers were scrubbed almost to
shining.
Testing day was important.
We were important.

Looking at the Hive kids, there were many thrown into our mix
with their drab gray uniforms, we felt ourselves to be luckier
than anyone in the world.
Only the grim Breaker, lounging lazily outside the Testing room
door
with an old-fashioned rifle in hand reminded us of the stakes.
I answered the questions the best I could, my mind seeming to
buzz in recognition.
I could do this.

This was what I had been training for.

Unfair, came the whine, often, after the exam,
in that hour lull while the answers were processed.
But I exulted in the silence, half-ashamed.

Lines of fresh-faced youngsters, with myself somewhere fidgeting
in the mix
with my too-big blouse and my insipid hair-ribbons.
The lone Breaker in gleaming black uniform stood in the center
of this sea of youth,
a large assortment of bowls filled with white paper slips set out
on the table beside him.
One by one, he read the number of each child, their test score,
their grouping, Palace or Camps, their segment of each and their
class within their society, and their eventual profession.
Out of each of the bowls, split by Palace or Camps and into
their segments, he would read their new names. Every so often,
he would call out a number but no score
and the boy or girl called would be grouped into the corner.
The boy in front of me was trembling with nervousness,
dark hair plastered to his head in a shiny black cap.

The Breaker easily shifted his weight and read from his scroll:
Number 2786. Score: High in Reading and Critical Analysis.
Low in Mathematics. Low in Scientific Induction. High in
Vocabulary. Low in Practical Application. High in Writing.
Grouping: Camps. Segment: Writer's Camp. Class: Second
Tier. Profession: Copy Writer, Health Corps.
The boy seemed to sag with relief.
Completely ignoring this, the Breaker took his time fishing
about in the Writer's Camp, Second Tier bowl. He pulled out a
paper slip, and read off the name Hearst.

It was my turn.

Number 2346. Score: Fair in Reading Comprehension and
Critical Analysis. High in Mathematics. High in Scientific
Induction. High in Vocabulary. High in Practical Application.
High in Writing.
Accusing eyes turned to me as the Breaker paused.
He asked me if I knew my choices, and I could only nod
numbly.
High scores or close to it across the board gave you a few
choices.
I could choose the Palaces and live a life of comfort, but I would
never see my family again.
I could choose the Camps, but that would only give my mother
a permanent mouth to feed.
Or…I could be a Breaker.
Taking on the black uniform would allow my mother and my
brother until his Testing Day
to move into a Breaker village, which wasn't luxurious, but
guaranteed enough to eat.

My mouth opened before I could stop it and by the time I spoke
it was too late.
The Breaker cleared his throat.
Number 2346. Score: Fair in Reading Comprehension and
Critical Analysis. High in Mathematics. High in Scientific
Induction. High in Vocabulary. High in Practical Application.
Grouping: Breaker. Segment: First Tier. Class: New Watchman
(subject to change)
Profession: Written Camps Patrol.

No name for me, but a casual nod in my direction and a
number, Breaker (Watchman) 256.
Probationary.

That is it. That's how it happened.
Nothing particularly dramatic, or noteworthy.
I plodded to my fate like a cow to the slaughter
with the endless song of unfair ringing in my ears.

A choice that wasn't a choice. What else could I have done?

BLUE

My poor fool.

What perfectly crafted arrogance in the face of an artificial night!

It is always dark in the Barracks save for the electric lights that
line the corridors,
but I had at reading that first sentence an urgent need of a
candle
to burn those words into dust and ashes—

Images of an aristo.

Third channel on our television sets constantly tuned to the
smiling-faced advertisements
or at times important announcements, the first memories of
these superiors.
Galileo, Human Services Coordinator, resplendent in gleaming
white robes,
his eyes wide and knowing.
We knew nothing of them save that we were as animals to them.
Smooth-skinned Artists in the advert industries, chosen for their
pallor
would tell us that our purpose was to become more like them,

even though we knew that that would be impossible.
There were contacts on sale in the Pharmacies for those Artists who could
scrounge to afford them, damaging their eyes to get that deep mysterious look,
and lead-based foundation to lighten skin after a life of toil.
And it was in that moment as I read the mocking words that said that his true belief
was that all effort on his part would fail, I hated him.
I hate him far more than I had ever hated an aristo
and that hatred only continues to intensify the further I read.

All for the love of an Author.
Descartes?

I can sense his self-awareness and it drives my blood cold.
Aristos are not meant to feel pity.
They are not meant to sense their differences or their gradations of genius.
They are not meant to know that anything that they were doing was wrong.
That, in a sense, is their main redeeming quality,
the one thing that removes them from true human horror.
To save or to kill is meant to be equal to them.
That was the myth that had been spread since the beginning,
and that was supposed to be our sole source of hatred and of pity.
True, the aristos have the intelligence that our society demands but all that brilliance comes at a significant price.
We are at their mercy, but at least we feel something, however brief, in our existence.
They were…are… not human.

They can feel neither hatred nor love, and the games that they
play with our lives are as meaningless and immature as a child
picking the wings off a fly.
They torture us not out of malice but out of alien curiosity.
To see how long it takes us to die.

And we were special in our ignorance, aristo-who-writes.

I wonder if this is not just an elaborate sham, if he was just
affecting emotion to get into my head or whatever unfortunate
reader would stumble upon his words.
I wonder if everything I saw had been a projection—
that half-tilt looking out past the curious crowd might have been
anything
from complete boredom to sudden hunger.
But no, sadness, I was sure of it.

Say what you like, aristos are not like us.

But they have families, mothers, fathers.
How could they when they were bred in a lab, a swab of cheek
cells?
How many infants bobbing in amber vials slumbering in
dreamless sleep?
You hear things as a writer employed to formulate the messages
of the Palaces,
but nothing like this.
Families? A new era of aristos? Were they outmoding
themselves?

Descartes. I almost chuckled at the presumption of it.

Past twenty years ago I would have leapt at the chance to take
another shot at a story.
It was almost as if he knew the journalist heart in me that pulsed
involuntarily
at the most sordid tale, the weapon that could exact the most
damage.
I thanked my lucky test scores I made it to translate the Aristo
message to the people.

I set a trap and penned the lies to the world.

What choice did I have?

What choice do I have?

The letter rests temptingly in my hands.
Five seconds more and it will lie torn into anonymity.
It was a cold December morning twenty years ago when last
words fell into my hands
and attempted to tear down a dynasty.
I trusted long ago in the power of those words and I ended up
here.
What was left for me without one last story?
What else exists for me but to again pick up the paper and the
pen?

BREAKER 256

The tests get harder every year for everyone, including new
Breakers,
but it doesn't stop there for the Watchmen.
First few weeks are always the hardest.
Your district group of prospective Breakers is brought to the
Palaces by your overseeing Breaker where you undergo a
physical evaluation overseen by norm assistants.
If you pass that, you are put through a special series of exams in
the Citadel
to further test your mental acuity.
Failure in any examination results in execution.
If you pass the exams, you are permitted to go into training,
which involves first a ten-day stint in the Palace training fields
and gymnasiums.
You are given marginal food, water, and sleep.
Failure to keep up with training results in execution.
Pass initial training and you meet your first aristo.
For our section of Eden, we had Human Services Coordinator
Galileo
and Human Services Assistant Newton.
Who ever is Coordinator now, young Darwin, gives you your
initial beats.

Survive a year on all your assignments while wearing the red
uniform and you are given
an official badge with your number, a place in a Breaker village
with your kin, and a destiny.

I remember the glory of that day,
the freshness first off the training field, drenched in sweat and
blood.
There were only five survivors in my grouping, with 376 as one
of them.
I remember 376, the man who would become my shadow, and
far more.
How he did not smile when the uniforms were presented,
but wore his like a second skin.
We stood in a haggard line, gazing with veiled mistrustful eyes at
the mass of sleek Breakers watching us indifferently,
for they must have known that our suffering was far from over.
None of us were naive enough to believe that our lives would be
improved.
Not after testing in the Hives, not after our training.
But despite this, our weary hearts were heavy with the Duty,
and some fools such as me were filled with the fire
to serve to make the lives of our families better.
But all of us knew that we were traitors.
Every last one of us had been born into poverty in the Camps,
and we shivered there, at the center of the State
that had murdered our people.
We were guard dogs meant to run with the wolves.
But with your stomach full, a gun in hand loses its abhorrence,
and a traitor lives, if only as a traitor.

So I watched the Watchmen after my report.

I was in the house of Galileo, who sat gracefully
and watched the recruits on the training field with hooded eyes.
Sonnet's poetry still echoed in my mind, but I feared that he
could read my thoughts.
Sometimes Galileo watched me instead, as if he would speak.
He was beautiful in the synthetic light, and on his face I traced
lines that looked like my own.
I wanted to ask him how many Watchmen he thought would
survive,
but I did not open my mouth quickly enough.
His young child asked it for me.
Aristos are predominately male, but it took me a moment
to recognize the child is referred to as a boy.
The child, Darwin, moved with small, careful movements as he
constructed with rapidity
a perfect copy of the major Palace collection,
the Citadel and its clock-tower, out of interlocking blocks.
It was a casual question, a throw-away, and Galileo smiled a
sudden secret smile.
Outside a Watchman lagged behind the group, and a shot rang
briefly out upon the air.

As many as deserve to, he responded, and his long hand ruffled
the hair of the child.

I still stood but for a gesture from Galileo and then I sat there at
his feet.
A strange rebellion had corroded my heart and sickened the feel
of his hand on my arm.
We are all somebody's dog, I thought, and the boy looked up at
me

with eyes as black as ink, no whites at all.

I looked at the lines of hopeful and doggedly obstinate
Watchmen marching out there on the fields, and the one cast to
the side, so small and so still.
How many would be left for the next day?

Tomorrow, tomorrow, and tomorrow, I said quietly,
and Galileo glanced at me with wild dark suspicion.
He asked where I heard it, came by it.
I called it foolishness.
A rash deed, I assured him, and he turned his head.
He could not have heard it, then.
Breaking the Censor would be madness.
Almost as bad as kill a king.
As kill a king.
As kill a King.

FLASHOVER

BLUE

Words with a man on Cleaning Day.
Shivering in the January cold, I stare steadily ahead at the man
in front of me
who on that fateful day had passed me the letter.
His sickness has worsened, lesions puckering his skin, his eyes
blank as two marbles.
I wait expectantly for my letter and when it comes down the
line
I grab it and seize that moist hand.
I demand to know who passed me the letter, but his hand lies
limp and unresisting in my grip.
He ignores me.
I attempt to reason it out.
How could the aristo have communicated to his man that the
letter was for my eyes only?
How could his man know who I am?
Who was he?
And Descartes is dead.
So who is it now?
I growl in frustration, and ask if these letters, the first and the
last were always meant for me.
His eyes never bother to turn my way but the corner of his
mouth raises in a silent ironic smile.

"We all know who you are and what you have done."

My fingernails have dug crescent moons of blood into his palm.
I whisper furiously the importance of knowing my benefactor
and inquire if it is him,
but he only coughs weakly and smiles that sad little smile.
I hear a Breaker's shout and I drop the man's hand, folding up
my letter in fifths
and shoving it unceremoniously down into my uniform shirt.

The Palace car has gone, and the Cleaners wander unhurriedly
down the line.
The man in front of me turns his head to meet my eye.
He had passed the last elimination.
He would not pass another.

A plague-stick points towards the left and he is gone.

Who am I?

I thought I knew.

Gunshots in the distance.

I was a journalist, that much I was certain, although I was sure
that was not the title they would have used.
I was a promotion specialist.
I was hired for my lies, and for my words.
I could convince anybody of anything.
I had chosen my fate as much as anyone could in my time.
Confronted by an aptitude for numbers,

I had chosen to skew the scores, fail the science, choose the
Camps.
I doubt anyone ever knew, but I had long fancied myself a hero.
Now, here, in the damp and the snow, I'm not so certain,
and the woman that cleans my cell agrees.
It reminds me of someone I once loved,
and a smile that evaporated
like breath off a blade.

We all know who you are, she seemed to whisper, and he was
straight-backed as they led him off.
They never look back.
If that prisoner was right, then they all knew of my failure.

Tell me what you know, and the whispers sounded
of elegant instruments just asking to be used in a windowless
room.
Tell me what you know, and a prisoner I have never met asks me
for a name that is not mine.
Tell me what you know, servant of the State.
Twenty years ago, I watched the words die in the cold and the
snow, and did nothing.

I was happy to live.

I unfurl the letter in the privacy of my cell and turn the paper
over to note that it is another page of the booklet, and the Edict
number is *4563: The Exemption of Aristos.*
I turn it over again and folding out the corners with hands damp
with snow, begin to read:

SECOND LETTER

DESCARTES

To the Artist:
I see you received my letter.
So tell me what you know of Author.
That is the first thing everyone wants to know, isn't it?
Not of you, not of your accomplishments, but of the words
that died there in the December snow to general applause.
The world is a much darker and sinister place than you could have
ever imagined, my poor fool.
So now you know that the letter was originally meant for you.
Good.
Now is not the time for you to seek out and unravel the story of how
I got to know your identity,
or how I set this unusual series of plans in motion.
Rather, remember the words that died alone in the dark and the
snow.
Did you know that Author was part aristo?
At least half.
They all were, really, the Breakers.
Where do you think so many of them gained such a length of bone,
a quickness of speed,
a callousness of heart?
But that is a lie, isn't it?
We aristos were not bred to be exempt from empathy, we didn't
need to be.

All it took to butcher your people was not to think of them as people at all.
And none of you cared to raise a hand against us, not only out of fear, but out of pity.
You pitied us.
And out of pity, you exulted in your ignorance and your humanity.
Save for one.
Forty years ago a Breaker broke and began to spread the truth to the people.
Two decades later she was dead.
Or was she?
I have watched your career with great interest, and your life with greater interest in here.
I know who you are, and what you have done.
Author, The Martyr, she must be dead, but still the writings write on.
After her fall, it was you, taking up the pen.
But then you were sent here—
So who was it after then, Blue?
And who will it be now?

—Descartes

PART TWO: GROWTH

EDICT 5693: The Nation of Eden is lenient. If a man should prove to be treasonous, there will be a careful review. If convicted, that man will be imprisoned or else put to death.

BREAKER 256

And the Lady Justice stands at the top of the Barracks,
gazing down without expression on the parade grounds
where the Watchmen once marched, and now Cleaners stand
without moving.
The Lady is the last that stands from before the Censor.
She is Justice, but she is not our Justice.
She is Justice grown hideous with human frailty.
She watches the parade ground with blank medieval eyes over
the atrocities
with her sword outstretched, and scales,
due to mechanical flaw or irony,
tipped, and blindfold torn away.
She looks on benignly over the workhouses and the Hives,
the staccato of gunshots and the training of the Breakers,
and smiles a manufactured smile over the Barracks.
With her back to the people.
With her back to the Camps.

BLUE

And the Lady Justice stands at the top of the Barracks,
gazing down without expression on the parade grounds
where the Watchmen once marched, and now Cleaners stand
without moving.
The Lady is the last that stands from before the Censor.
She is Justice, and she was once my Justice.
She is Justice grown corrupted apart from morality.
She watches the parade ground with blank medieval eyes over
the atrocities
with her sword outstretched, and scales,
due to mechanical flaw or irony,
tipped, and blindfold torn away.
She looks on benignly over the dull pressure of beatings,
the staccato of gunshots and the acrid smoke of the burnings,
and smiles a manufactured smile over the Barracks.
With her back to the people.
With her back to the Camps.

BREAKER 256

A careless wave of a hand and I was dismissed for the time being.
It had been an uneventful week.
There had been two deaths in Poet's Camp
and one dramatic execution of a violinist by one of the inner-
camp gangs.
Five more deaths in the large section of Writer's Camp
sectioned off for Prose,
filthy water supply suspected.
Normal, everyday stuff and Galileo had long lost interest.
As I turned to leave, I saw that those black eyes,
the whites transparent as lace,
flickered to where my medal ought to be.
The thin mouth never spoke a word.
He rarely focused on my face, but I often looked at his, intent,
as if on a new species of animal.
Something about that thin, aristocratic face, with its elongated
bones, seemed so right.
It resonated in my being, as if I was plucked like a harp.
He smiled a fractured little smile.
I puzzled at its broken perfection and wondered what it meant,
that *hatred*,
when that freezing hand came to rest upon my arm like it did
upon the head of the child.
Confused, I waited in the silence that followed, his lips moved as
if about to speak,
*I loved it despite myself when he spoke, it was like torn velvet left to
rot in the street.*
But he only gave me a slip of paper that I recognized with
Eden's white oak seal.

I folded it and bowed my head.
"When next do you have need of me?"

"Tomorrow."

Home, and there was fire in the big black belly of the stove, and
my mother stood tending it.
I had not been home all week, but I came through the door of
our humble house
bearing food and bottled water like gifts.
I needn't have, we had enough.
I thought that this was strange and wanted to ask about the
sudden wealth of my mother,
humming at the stove.
But I did not.
My Breaker uniform and coat lay draped over a chair
in the bedroom that my brother and I shared.
In plainclothes, I shivered in front of the warmth, looking at my
little brother as
he laboriously went over problem sets in his CEE workbook.
I wish I could have given him a tutor.
Our schoolroom was there, in the warm kitchen with its too-
often scrubbed brown table.
We only sent him to regular classes at the next Hive when it
came close to mock exams.
He failed the last.
I searched his face as if trying to find anything of me in him,
and not succeeding,
I sat next to him and studied with him in front of the fire.
My brother was not the best at the mocks, but he had a genius
for words.

I used to find snippets of stories hidden in his drawers when he was younger,
fantastic stories full of heroes and villains and brave little kids.
The stories stopped since heavy CEE prep began, but I've kept every one of them.
He looked at me half-way through the set and then reached over to touch the side of my face.
He showed me his hand, a tiny drop of blood had smeared into powder.

"Are you hurt?"

"Someone else's."

He turned back to his workbook, satisfied.
Now that he was twelve and had come into contact with Breakers on the job,
I got the sense that he knew who and what I was.
He was good about it.
He didn't ask questions.
Sometimes I would come home and my uniform would be torn, bloodied,
burned,
gashed in a thousand different places, but he never asked about my job.

There was a hitch in the last problem, and I guided his progress with patient hands.

That night was the last night for my brother, because testing started the next day.

He could not stay here unless he had by a miracle tested and chosen into being a Breaker.
I did not want that for him.

One night, one test.

Late that night, as he climbed into our shared narrow bed, in our shared narrow room.
I wondered what it was that I could do for him, to give him something,
something that he could remember me by.
He was half asleep, turned away from me, when he spoke.

"Breaker 256. That's a funny name."

"Yes. It is a funny name. No funnier than yours, though. Child 3457."

"But I'll get a real one once I pass testing. You never will."

Once you pass testing.

"Yes, that's right."

"What should I call you, then? You can't just be another person."

I smiled in the darkness.
If only that were simple enough.
He waited for my answer, but I did not have one to give him.
Eventually, he spoke again, as if tired of my waffling.

"Well, what is it you do well?"

Well? I could track a man by recognizing his gait from any other man.

I could scale walls without equipment and could fire a pistol at long range and a stunner at short.

I knew a hundred different ways to kill a man without a weapon, and a thousand more with.

I could hide my fears and my sorrows from the most highly trained analysts in Eden.

I could withstand cold, hunger, rain and torture.

I could do all these things, but I am proud of none of them.

I stumbled upon a suitable answer.

"I can tell stories."

"What is a person who tells stories?"

Someone with a very short life expectancy, I thought, but I said—

"A writer. An author. A fool."

He seemed to think this over for a moment, and in this instant I felt the mad panic one feels if one is about to lose someone and I thought of the unthinkable, the Breaker in the classroom, the firing range, the heavy tread of a boot upon the stair.

What if he should fail?

"Tell me a story then, Writer-author-fool."

I held him close in the darkness and paused.
"It won't be a very long story '34. What do you want it to be about?"

"Anything you like."

"How about a fire?"

COMET

I stood in the line, my pencil was broken in my grip, my ears
filled with buzzing.
Mechanically, the Breaker lifted the scroll, read the score,
grabbed the names, read them aloud.
I was numb to all that, all but the memory of the exam.
My thoughts had been like lightning, the test giving up all its
answers to me, carefully revealed.
I was saved.
Safe.
56859.
I looked for my friend among the crowd, the faces began to
blend, more faces than names.
I looked for the thin kid with hair that was far too short and
eyes that were far too bright.
I saw nothing.
No one.
My turn.
I slowly stepped forward and the Breaker read my score.
Number 56409. Score: Fair in Reading and Critical Analysis.
High in Mathematics. High in Scientific Induction. Low in
Vocabulary. High in Practical Application. Low in Writing.
Grouping: Palaces. Segment: Management. Class: First Tier.
Profession: astrological research and promotion (probationary).
Proposed assignment: Health Corps.
I stumbled from the line with my new name ringing in my ears.
Comet.
My name is Comet.
There was a bright future in front of me.
The world is too bright.

I stumbled and fell to my knees, I was searching, but I forgot for
what.
Faces.
His face was not among the others, grouped into their
segments,
brand new lives of useful service stretching out in front of them.
I could not find him, I cannot—
The book. The book he gave me.
In case, he said.
A heavy hand yanked me to my feet, and led me to the Palace
grouping where I foundered.
In case of what?
Idiocy tattooed in bright ink.
I was almost alone.
The three other kids meant for the Palaces looked down at me
with disdainful eyes
and I finally stopped searching.
There was only one place that he could have been.
By then they had led the failures from the room.
My name is Comet,
Comet: a celestial body, moving about the sun—
and my best friend is dead.

THE CENSOR

Once upon a time, there were the books and the fire but first there were the people. And out of the people came the labs, and out of the labs came the aristos but before that there was the judging. Too many people, they said and some were not contributing. Worse than that, some were spreading dangerous ideas. There were not many books then, but they were the only thing that could not be regulated. So they doled out technology to those who would be in the Palaces.

And for the rest, they burnt the books.

They said that they could not create a new world upon the foundation of the old, as they would always be reminded of their past mistakes. But they could create a new world out of the ashes of the old, so they built a big bonfire in the winter Citadel, where the white oak of Eden now stands. And on the bonfire, they threw the books and watched them get consumed by the fire. This was the Censor, when the world's history went up in flames.

There was no crying that day, only joy. And how they danced around the fire, and laughed and made their jokes. And after the world's history had been burnt and they had raked the ashes, they planted a single oak tree. The tree of knowledge grew and grew, but its branches were as white as the ashes.

PART TWO: GROWTH (Cont.)

COMET

A new world was before me,
but I do not want it.
The world beyond my Hive was far too bright.
For the first time in days I could see the sky.
Snow fell like discouraged birds
that were too weak to fly.
I had never felt snow.
It was cold to the touch.
Transient.
It covered the sidewalks and dotted the synthetic black coat of
my Breaker,
376.
The big man strode ahead of us to meet the curb, and
the Palace car with its mirrored windows.
From the muzzle of his mask came the steam of his breath
like a great medieval dragon,
rifle slung casually over his shoulder as if he expected not to use
it.
I stood by his side, watching the car reach us in the silence,
and his heavy hand that still had blood under the fingernails
held mine.
Comfort.
I was not meant to find him beautiful.

His eyes were steady and certain behind his mask.

New world.
New life.

But the others, they did not speak.
Despondently, they watched the cruiser whisper up to the curb
and we were ushered inside.
I rested my head against the rich leather of my seat
and could not look upon the world as it passed.
So I closed my eyes
and I thought of the last tale told to me in my Hive.
What did 376 know?
He looked out the window beside me
and watched the world go by.
He rarely spoke, and less often smiled but
it was as if he knew something.
We knew not to fight against Eden.
That had been attempted and failed, so many years ago.
Author.
The broken Breaker.
Eden's enemy, the one that attempted to take down the State
through words.
Her name is in our history trainers along with all the other
traitors.
They told us.
It is because of her and the Artist that the testing is more
stringent.
It is because of her that the children die.
56859, another casualty.
A long time ago, there were hints of revolutions.
But none have happened since.

For they are too afraid, I think.

The Artists.

They are so afraid and so alone, and they think that they owe
them,

that they own them,

that they owe them so much.

BLUE

Author.
Yes, I know a lot about Author.
Too much some days, haunting my head.
Only fragments of a picture in my mind, pale skin, dark eyes,
beautiful hands.
Enemy, friend, lover.
In the Barracks when all the lights are out, I hear the cries of the
men that she sent there,
and try to think of anything of her but that last day.
Try.
Try to remember.
Remember the delicate hands that paused at thinking,
the serious aristocratic face that so rarely cracked into a smile.
Strength, certainty, the light behind her head.
Anything, anything but—
the words that died in the cold and snow.
Alone at the window, gazing over the crowd that had gathered,
so still and so forgotten.
And then she turned her head and laughed.
There, at the failing of a revolution, she laughed.
The one eye not put out by the brand sparkled with obscene
confidence.
There was so much scarring, so much damage to the right side
of her face,
the brand of Eden's tree of knowledge snaking over her pale
skin,
over the face that had been so beautiful that it had hurt to look
at her, like the sun.
It hurt to look at her.

She was always beautiful, but beautiful like a fire is beautiful,
not to be touched.
I touched her then, the skin that had been salvaged from the
brand and from the fire
and I asked her why.
I was only sixteen.
I had only just learned to put pen to paper.
I had been hired to destroy her, to share the lies, to refute the
truths that she had bared
in all their hideousness to the world.
I had been happy enough to play the dog at Galileo's feet,
and now all I had to do was tell the world that she had been
right
and that I had been wrong,
but I was so frightened and so alone.
Forty years ago, a Breaker broke and shared the truth with the
world.
Twenty years ago I killed her with my words.
It was for Eden. It was—
All I can remember of her this instant, the broken creature in
the fractured winter sunlight,
and she had been so beautiful.
It was in December, and it was in the snow.
I stood in the crowd, the crowd was jeering, the crowd was
angry.
I was silent while a battered Galileo took the podium, stretching
out those wide hands for silence.
The distant figure of my Author stood without speaking,
sandwiched between 376 and another Breaker, a gun to her side,
to her ruined face.
I expected a struggle, but the chained hands never moved.

And Galileo said:

"I give you your hero."

And the outrage poured over.

This was it?

This half-aristo shivering in the winter sunlight, listening to her sentence,

the oak tree of Eden seared into an implacable face?

Treason. Lies.

The world was looking at her with its full hatred,

but that single dark eye was looking out into the crowd,

waiting, expecting me to come forward, and humble enough to hope.

I could not look her in the face.

For the last words that I had—

But Galileo said:

"Is there anyone here who objects to this sentence?"

I had rehearsed this moment in my mind.

Eden might fall.

I struggled between my love and a nation.

But a decision then made—

I would break from the crowd, run up to the balcony,

and tear her from the Breakers' deadly embrace.

We would escape the Palaces, I would take her back, clean her wounds, fill out her gaunt frame, get her to smile again, allow her to craft the words.

I would tell the world that I had betrayed her, that I had been alone

and had owed the aristos so much, that I had been afraid.

And I would accept the consequences.

But I said:

Nothing.

Remember. Remember. Remember.
But
I was so afraid and so alone, and I owed them so much.

BREAKER 256

I sat silently in the darkness of a Palace car, the outline of a
stunner gun pressing into my ribs.
The Breaker beside me regarded me impassively, his features
hidden behind his black mask,
his eyes behind tinted glass windows.
The stunner gun's barrel dug in further and I smiled in the
darkness.
Shoot, I told him.
He did not answer, nothing but the flash of his eyes behind the
mask.
I would taunt him no longer, the exhilaration of being alive had
worn off
and had been replaced by tedium and apprehension.
376 had done his work with an Artist's touch.
My entire body ached from industrial boots, my ribs were
bruised,
my face swollen and bleeding sullenly from a hundred different
places.
I smiled at nothing, and the expression cut into my pain and left
a ghost.
Alive. I am alive.
And I looked like the monster I am.
No memories but fractured thoughts, I never remember the
pain.
Except, perhaps the sound of someone screaming, far off beyond
the darkness.
Yes.
Perhaps that.

I was a fool to think that Galileo wouldn't find out about my
exploit in Poet's Camp,
and in a way, I wanted him to find out.
Too obvious.
376.
He must have stayed behind.
His guilt and my sentence were written in those steady dark
eyes.
I knew. Of course I knew.
I wanted an audience for my pointless rebellion
and I got the most attentive one I could have wanted.
Galileo.
My biggest fan.
Fractured pictures and I was looking into eyes of mercy, the
light of a single light bulb
reflecting in his gaze like a perfect coal of hate.
Tell me everything.
And I did.
I did.
They had found my medal melted down in the possession of
three unrelated Artists.
The little girl I gave it to was found in a ditch in Writer's Camp.
Her throat had been cut.
I must have started laughing there in the darkness.
Remorse, even here, right here where I was supposed to die?
And I reached up a hand to touch that pristine face, vandalizing
with my blood
that face that shone out like a blasphemy.
How marvelous.
How trite.

But I am, I am alive, for reasons that I cannot, will not
understand.

The Breaker gripped my arm and led me out to my destination.
The clatter of school-children. The ring of a bell.
Down the gray corridor, down in the Hive.
It was testing day, it was testing day.
376 was there, at his post.
He saw the damage once more that he had done
at Galileo's urging
but could only put a rifle into my hands for comfort.
He read from a scroll, the numbers unfamiliar save for one.
I could not think. I could not feel.
I was taken around the back.
The rifle was heavy in my hands.
My thoughts were fog, a gun was at my side,
and I could not comprehend that—
The face of a marvel and a voice of velvet discarded to rot in the
street.
I have need of you.
When?
Tomorrow.
But the children. The children.
The children were lined up, facing the back wall.
I could not see their faces.
I was—
I am—
resigned.
I turned to 376 and asked for a mask.
No mask, he said, and cocked his gun.
I stepped forward with the rifle, his gun was at my back.

The other Breaker watched from the doorway to pick me off if I tried to run.

I would not.

I would not run.

I stepped down the line and fired with my eyes half-closed.

Just percussion sounds, I told myself.

Not gunshots at all.

No blood.

Just children, children made of straw.

I willed myself to stop breathing.

Just four more. Just—

I should have gone, should have turned to run, should have been gunned down there in the sunlight, should have slipped and fallen in the blood of children.

But I did nothing.

I fired down the line and I willed myself dead.

Three.

Two.

One.

I could not think. I could not feel.

And the last, my brother, he said the words for me, as he always has.

"Will it hurt?"

"No."

And I fired in time to catch him in my arms.

In that last second he had turned his head to see me, and I held him in the sunlight.

I cannot think. I cannot feel.

But there must have been tears, the salt stung my face and I remember.

I remember.

But I was so afraid and so alone, and I owed them so much.

Aftermath. Emptiness.

I had been put under probation, close watch, not to return home.

My mother sat alone in our little house,

the news of my brother's failure played on the third channel by midnight.

I see her now, threadbare robe wrapped, sitting on a threadbare couch.

Galileo mounted the podium, elegant and slim in robes that were too small for him,

and read the names.

He always read the names in tones of perfect solemnity, referred to them as the fallen,

but his eyes gleamed as if he were laughing,

and my mother was alone.

As I was when they took my brother away from me.

It took both Breakers to tear him from my arms, just long enough to see that my bullet,

that my bullet was true.

376 had held me for a very long time.

I had kept my promise.

It didn't hurt.

It didn't—

And the rain, the rain washed his blood away, I was clean enough for the Palaces.

Galileo was waiting for me.

Me.

His bruised and broken Breaker so ill at ease in his gleaming reception room where the walls shone like mirrors and others stood handsome in their sleek black uniforms.

I fell at his feet and his hands came to cup the face

that he had beaten and bruised so mercilessly.

They were cool like marble and far off, far off the voice of a small child crying in relief.

"Kill me," that small voice said, the voice I could not, would not recognize as my own.

He gazed at me in silence and there was something like affection in those still, opal eyes.

"Is that what you want? Think now. You wanted so badly to live."

I sagged in those elegant hands.

"I-I was…I was so afraid—"

"Of course you were."

Eyes hypnotizing, their pupils expanding and contracting, the hands caressing.

"Will it solve all your problems, my Breaker? Will you see your brother again?

If I kill you now, will all your pain go away?"

A smile like a sliver of ice wedged itself into my heart.

"You are in pain, aren't you?

Five seconds away from throwing yourself on the funerary pyre.

And you wish… you wish that I would burn you.

Like an injured dog that crawls back to its master, you beg for me to let it go all away."

I reached weakly forward.

"I…I…"

The smile sharpened.

"No.

In the end, we are all someone's dog.

You will live for me. You will stay for me. You will remember—"

"For you," I whispered, and my hatred was complete.

"No.
For you, Breaker.
That is your punishment. I condemn you to be you for the rest of
your life."

BLUE

Beginnings, the farewell of a Hive, and I had exalted in my own cleverness.

I failed the numbers, won the words, and subsequently, my life.

I cannot remember my exact score, but I thought that I had beaten them, tricked the system.

What a fool I was.

To think that I could shake off the Camps.

I am no longer part of the people.

Released to the Palaces under the watchful eyes of aristos that we thought were Gods.

And they were, they are—

Cruel as we all would be, were we gods.

And the filth of the Camps was washed away
by Galileo's gleaming hand.

Author, why did you ever wish to return to it?

Those hollow-eyed people skulking in the streets.

How could you call yourself one of them?

I was freed.

Freed from ignorance.

Freed from pain.

Freed from hunger.

But you would have said that I bargained my soul.

For gold is worth more than silver.

I still remember my first glimpse in person of an aristo,
my first sight of Galileo rising to meet my escorts.

Still in gray uniform, darned by the female prisoners in the Factory,

I marveled at the bright new world that shining marble had promised me.

He was handsome, but it was an alien handsomeness,
a glimpse of something magnificent and unaccountably strange.
It was so different, seeing him in person, the tallness and the thinness,
the warmth and chill of each expression.
He glided across the gleaming floor to meet us and we were in the presence of a king.
It is hard to explain, the relationship between the norms and the aristos.
But we did not hate them, not at first.
And he is—was—so beautiful.
He looked down at me in my torn Hive uniform from that lofty height and I fell in love.
There is no other way to describe it, the power that a great one, one of the leaders has over you.
There is warmth and calm, it is like meeting an angel, and those eyes, those eyes are so far away.
So immensely indifferent to human suffering and pain, and never knowing fear,
twinkling as the stars gleam somewhere long past the city lights.
I knew instantly that he saw me only as an insect on a slide,
a creature whose death throes would at worst be tedious and at best amusing,
but I had fallen in love, and love makes you blind.
Name. Score. Assignment.
He had addressed the Breakers instead of me
and for the first time in my life I saw them, really *saw* them.
Descartes, his poisonous words... but I knew.
I knew they must be part of it all, on the side of these angels.
But the Breakers, the monsters that mothers threatened their children with humor and more than a little fear, these boogeymen in the dark, they were human and they were alone.

I met the eye of a scarred one across the way that had been
watching our little entourage with lazy disinterest and was
rewarded with a smile that evaporated like breath off a blade.
Who were they then, these faces?
Did they not feel what I felt, there at that moment?
So I stood, quiet and alone, before the giant, the writer with the
Second-Tier Painter name, overpopulation incarnate.
But in those eyes and that benignly smiling face
I saw the problems of the ages wiped gently away.
And he was like a being, a being of light, so pure and so
beautiful,
but beautiful in the way that ice is beautiful,
all brilliant rainbows and facets, without the burden of heat.
His hand on my shoulder was insubstantial as a snowflake.
They are cruel, aristos, as we all would be were we gods,
without the fear of morality or time.
But he smiled and told me
"Welcome home."
And I was lost.
I was lost.

COMET

The first time,
I met a monster.
It was in the Palaces
and dressed in the clothes of an angel.
This was an aristo?
The perfect male animal,
and I heard that they are beautiful.
I saw him on the television, third channel, and he was—
His eyes were the eyes of a shark rolled over.
His skin was pock-marked, the shade of an eggshell crushed
beneath the heel of a king.
Galileo.
The acknowledged savior of Eden from the scourge of the
words.
Nothing more, nothing to say.
Name. Score. Assignment.
And his child, Darwin, smiled, his eyes are black, with no whites
at all.
His growing child took my hand in his, with those elegant,
dangerous fingers, to lead me on,
past Galileo, the petulant child-king, it would have been unwise
to ruin his fun.
And the tall shape, as I left, with its mouth slashed into its face
like parchment
stood to full height.
Told me of its pride of me.
Its hopes of me.
And it knew my new name.
This thing in the Palaces, this old deceiver,

it knew my name.
Its words were human, its voice was soft, soothing, as delicate as
cat's claws snagging fabric.
I looked around me and found everyone taken in, as if blinded
by the beauty of this thing
that shone like the sun, this thing that masqueraded as an angel.
This monstrous thing that cavorted in the sunlight, and one
dead eye folded down
in a grotesque wink, as if it knew all the secrets of the world.
It knew that I could see—
He was beautiful, this aristo, but beautiful like a tragedy,
a cheap veneer that can be gently pried away.
And what was hidden behind the mask—
Darwin, all adolescent gangling and welling black eyes, tugged
me away.
I am not meant to find him beautiful.
As I went about the corner, I saw the tall shape bend
and reach one hand around to wave a slow goodbye.
Learn, Galileo told me.
"See what you can see."
And I did.
I did.

BREAKER 256

Books of the Edicts, condensed, helped reorganize my priorities.
I read in the Palaces long and late into the night but in the
Human Services public library,
my sources were limited.
On the wall above the single shelf, a smug Artist, hired for her
graceful propositions
and oblique dark eyes guaranteed a higher score
across targeted areas on the CEE for a month in tutor's care.
A week.
Galileo had graciously given me a week on probation from
work,
leaving me with more free time than I knew what to do with.
I spent my time healing, a hired norm from Health Corps at
my beck and call.
He was supposed to keep track of my feeding times to make sure
that I was not starving myself, and to avoid the conflict, I
managed to eat a small amount each day.
I passed my days in a kind of haze, allowing my hired man to
paint on the salve,
eating the tasteless gruel fed to all valuable invalids,
and writing letters to my mother that she would never receive.
All times I was not followed, I ended up there.
"What are they, these scars?"
And an aristo, Descartes, sat across from me, with his small
careful movements.
I was startled, I didn't hear him come in.
He was a stranger, a background figure, an expensive piece of
the menagerie,
but I recognized his pedigree.

It is easy to tell, the way they hold their heads.
He reached, traced a facial mark to its source, its tributaries.
"What reason, what crime?"
I started at his ignorance of my tragedy and his flesh that was
like marble but
his black eyes were warm, and there were small crinkles around
the edges
where he had smiled far too much.
I had never been so close to another aristo before save for Galileo
and Newton,
and had learned all about might and majesty.
This was different.
I could feel the strange heart beating.
"Your crime," he questioned again, his eyes flashing as if in
recognition,
and my answer was pulled, unmeaning, from the darkness.
"Love."
"Love," he repeated, puzzled, the voice of a man forgetting a
dream upon waking
and he stood as if to put his jacket about my quaking shoulders.
When you can't remember—
to love is to forget.
And then, embracing me, were arms of sheathed ice and a voice
like a violin
gathering and releasing all the sadness in the world.
"It's all right."
A whisper. A smile.
"I know now. I know who you are, and what you have done."
And in the concave chest his strange heart beat for something
other than me.
I am not myself.

But
I cannot remember how I was before.

BLUE

I had been four years in the Citadel before I spoke to her.
The light was gleaming about her dark hair like a slipped halo as
she stood alone,
watching the arterial Watchmen in their neat ranks.
Order. Precision.
Was she different?
Breaker 256.
Different from the rigid silent lines of Breakers in the
Palaces, shining uniforms,
a world hidden behind a face as smooth as stone?
No, she was not different, but she was alone.
The deep-set eyes were so far away.
Standing there like a statue long worn by wind and rain,
she would outlast us all.
But she turned to go as I approached,
a sixteen-year-old boy stammering in the snow.
And in desperation I grabbed her arm to stay her
and for the first time she looked at me.
The delicacy, the randomness of the scars across her forehead
and cheekbones stopped me,
the white-trails of some long ago tragedy.
Still forgotten.
"I know you," I said, and watched the dark eyes flicker like
flame.
"I don't think so."
But I did, and I do.
The tired Breaker watching my initiation with disinterest,
the smile that evaporated so quickly it was almost as if I had
imagined it.

"My initiation," I told her, not relinquishing my grip, and her
gaze was amused,
the corner of her mouth lifting slightly in the crooked half-smile
I remembered.
"I remember. Promotion specialist. But how do you—?"
"Your scars," and the smile faded as if struck from her face.
Images of her then, how she had watched and waited,
the only one who shrank back from Galileo's glance.
She tugged her arm gently out of my grip and began to walk
away.
I ran after her, panting, to keep up with her long strides.
She did not turn her head.
"Go away."
Stubbornly, I jogged by her side.
"Not until you tell me your name."
"Breakers don't have names. Everyone knows that."
"Then I have to write one for you."
I reached for her again.
She stopped in mid-stride, her dark eyes blazing, one hand going
for the stunner gun
I was certain was concealed beneath her coat.
I opened my arms, my chest free for aiming.
"Shoot," I told her, but she did not answer.
Nothing but the flash of fiery eyes in a face as pale as snow.
Finally she dropped her hand from her weapon, turned her head
and asked me,
"Why?"
My answer sprung to my lips without thought.
"Because you can't just be another person."
Silence, and we regarded each other.
Her eyes were focused on an indiscriminate point far off in the
distance,

105

occasionally darting back to me as if afraid.

I drank in everything about her with the eyes of an Artist, her graceful proportions and

fragile, helpless hands, hands of a woman of leisure that were never meant for a gun.

I moved a step forward and she flinched away.

"I won't hurt you."

She uttered a short laugh and told me to:

"Go home. Write your little lies, but spare them to me. This is no place for a child like you."

"My name is Blue."

I faced her then, searching her eyes for a hint that I had gotten through that formidable exterior.

I searched for her heart.

"Blue. A painter's name."

Another broken smile.

"Even your name is a lie."

"What could you possibly want from me?"

Nothing. Everything.

"You."

BREAKER 256

Home.

My mother slept on the threadbare couch, her knees drawn up to her chest.

She looked like a child, and when I kissed her cheek and pulled over the blanket,

she stirred, half-forgetting.

"34, is that you?"

"No," I told her, and she shifted slightly.

She must had been near asleep, her breathing was slow and even.

She would not

could not

remember.

"When is he coming home," she mumbled, and I soothed her, tucking the blanket under her chin.

"He is not coming home."

I watched the static dance on the television set and looked to nothing.

There was food in the house that I had not brought home.

My pay was late, and halved from my disgrace.

I never knew where she had gotten it,

and she was thin, thin enough to feel her bones

and not a fair opponent.

But it was empty, empty, without him and I sat there on the couch with my mother as she slept and I watched the static dance and I remembered.

Long ago, there was a man named Shakespeare, whose words were like music,

but most of his work was burned in a fire.

Descartes said to remember.

And I searched among our meager possessions
to find paper and a pen.
I found a pen, but no paper.
Nothing for my words.
But here, I found my brother's CEE workbook.
It was still on the table, and I tore out an empty page to write on
the back,
to compose my words.
My new assignment in the Hives was so soon.
Descartes.
One day we shall be together
but until then,
I wrote my words.

COMET

I did not sleep in my brand new bed.
The next day started my training.
Outside, there was only the hum of a stunner and the gentle toll
of the clock-tower.
I had never been close to it before, it is so loud.
Loud as the world, and Galileo whispered the night-time edicts,
canned sound bites for a busy man after the death of Newton.
That was not mentioned, the rebellions, the failings.
All memory that exists was hidden, lest it happen again.
Author.
Such legends, it is as if she never existed.
Still she wrote,
as if come back from the dead,
but nobody knew who it was.
Darwin, the son of Galileo, the new aristo with the all-black
eyes.
He told me that he saw the body executed for the people
afterward.
If it had been Author, the Breakers had done good work, he
said.
If it had been Author!
Half her face had been blown off by a close range rifle.
She was unrecognizable,
and it was for the best.
Everybody thought that she was a traitor.
So many had been killed in the chaos she created
that no one knew how to react when the writings started again.
The body that could have been anyone's.
There again, urging a rebellion.

as if come back from the dead.

First night in the Palaces and I was alone.
I was used to sleeping in the company of others,
the nonsense chatter, the breathing, the thousand petty
tragedies.
But I was alone, so I took out my booklet of Edicts
and read by faint electric light as if that would keep me safe.
I have kept the booklet, hidden it, treasured it,
and the handwriting of my friend fills up the slender margins.
Somewhere within the pages is a dark-haired boy smiling.
I told him he was clever, and that he was not to worry.
He told me I was silly and ran off to join the line.
I wondered what he felt when they put the gun to his head
in the line with the others, like vegetables ready for reaping
and if it was what she might have felt in those last moments.
But was she dead?
And did she die?
The writings—
Knowing that this was it,
that this second was the one for the ages.
I imagined him straight-backed for the blast.
Some of them plead and cry and kick when they are led from
the ceremony
to the retest and death.
But I am certain that he was straight-backed
and thought of poetry.

BREAKER 256

Au clair de la lune
Mon ami
Descartes.
Prête-moi ta plume
Pour écrire un mot.
Ma chandelle est morte
Je n'ai plus de feu.
Ouvre-moi ta porte
Pour l'amour de Dieu.

I think, therefore I am, Descartes,
I knew your namesake because you knew it.
Long ago a Frenchman died, and there you stood.
But where is France?
Where words are like music in a darkened room, like the twitter
of birds.
And does it exist still, far off beyond the boundaries of Eden?
I dream of a world where France exists,
and the people speak like birds.
You showed me your writings, and so many poems and works
from the hidden library in the Palaces,
the one locked with the heavy deadbolts and guarded by
Breakers.
You copied them down in your careful hand, as if you had to
think carefully about every word.
All these entities, like specters from the past,
Yeats, Shakespeare, Dante, Dumas, Hearst, Hugo, Tolkien, so
many,

and you spoke each name like a prayer, in reverence to these
dead men.
You knew of the world before the Censor because Galileo knew
it,
and he told you everything.
But what if I had told you, Descartes, that I hated your father,
Galileo,
that I sought to destroy him?
Would I have earned another of those lost looks,
or would you have urged me regardless to take up the paper and
the pen?
You taught me all that you knew.
What the world was.
Is.
What is a sonnet?
What is music, beyond a word?
I had told you of my fears of the world.
In three days after my week, I had been reassigned,
but you promised me you would not leave me.
We would meet when I came back to the Palaces.
I came back often.
You would not forget.
You will not betray me.
How will I remember that there is a world beyond the Breakers?
To remember is to write.
To forget is to love.
And I loved you, Descartes.

But enough to put aside the pen?

I think, therefore I am.
But

I do not think of you.
Instead
I think of the souls that danced in the cold and in the snow,
and lost
so many, many fires ago.

DESCARTES

To the Artist:
Tell me how much you know, and if it is a lie.
You will not tell?
Ah, then, well.
You are so tedious.
Coy.
Predictable.
Refusing to play our little game.
But how are you enjoying it, Artist?
And tell me the truth, although I know that it must be difficult for
you.
How far have you gotten in untangling my web?
We both know of Author, that is certain,
and that I cannot be Descartes.

Now Descartes is finally dead.
They put a bullet through his head.

But it suits so well, really, to use his name.
To be for once the aristo-who-writes.
Tell, fill in the gaps for me.
How she did it.
How she shared the words.
I know that you betrayed her.

And in return I will start again the revolution
to bring you back to the winning side.
Once more.
For your Author.
For she was right was she not?
The glory of the revolution,
the story of the people,
that there is only one side
that is on the side of the angels.
Descartes is dead, but I live on.
Do I seem like an angel?
Who am I?
Careful.
Watch the line.
And
do not shoot the messenger.

—Descartes

PART THREE: BLOSSOM

EDICT 6706: The Government of Eden is trusting. If a man should prove to be a perjurer and an equivocator, there must be evidence of his wrongdoings. If the evidence proves sound, that man will be imprisoned or else put to death.

If the right arm offends, cut it away.

AUTHOR

"Teach the ignorant as much as you can;
Society is culpable in not providing a free education for all
And it must answer for the night which it produces.
If the soul is left in darkness sins will be committed.
The guilty one is not he who commits the sin,
but he who causes the darkness."

—*Victor Hugo "Les Misérables"*

BREAKER 256

I never should have loved.
There was once a moment when I trusted
that the world was strange,
that the world was unfair
and that I was to be alone.
I am no different from them, Descartes.
I did what I had to do.
I am a measure in uniform,
I am a mind without a heart,
a bullet in a gun and
a footfall upon a stair.
I am a monster, Descartes.
And without the guilt that consumes me
all I could note is your white face in the darkness
with your shattered lips and silent eyes.
Your cold arms in the darkness were always mine.
And I was home.
Home,
and then our baby boy.
Our pure infant fire
that squalled and shook in
his makeshift cradle.
Our terrifying angel,
dark-haired, and like
an Artist born.
You protected me,
and our son,
had him sent to the Hives
and the child stalled a rebellion.

Twelve years, our promise charred upon your lips.
Wait until the child is grown
so he cannot be used against you.
Wait until he can take his chances.
Descartes.
I waited.
I waited too long.

And when the twelve years had passed
and our son was grown.
I stayed in the Palaces.
I read the works of dead men.
You had smuggled out the saved words of the ages
from the forbidden library.
Piece by piece under a jacket that was too small for you.
Only three books on the first day.
And I transcribed the words in my own handwriting,
the works of Genius lessened by my hand, their references
tainted.
Milton spoke of angels and of Eden,
the tree of knowledge, our death by,
our lives in the words of men who are dead.
Hugo wrote of rebellion and extremists,
and Shakespeare wrote plays.
But what of France, of England, of Angel-land
that kingdom of Angels
sunk under the sea, or conquered?
What of the world before the fire?
I wrote late
on slips of paper torn from my brother's CEE workbook
He would save them.
Prepared names.

Destinies of children.
My new position was in the Hives,
so I would remember,
the life-determined and the executioner.
I cannot think, I cannot feel.
But the words, and my words, make it back to the Camps
in the hands of those children who survive.
For I would give them not only a name, but a future.
There are some there who yet remember,
though most still try to forget.
The Citadel controls all higher technology.
What we did was the only way.
Galileo, unknowing, had given me my chance.
I had no intention of wasting it.
I would have salvaged the books that last from the fire.

Why, then?

The bartering of a life?
A life for words.
No meaning.
For one day, the Camps will say,
we will be dead.
But not today.
We are not dead today.

BLUE

The books that last from the fire,
and yet I cannot remember them.
It happened before I was born,
and I no longer crane to look along the line for my letters.
On Cleaning Day.
On Cleaning Day.
Close call today, I've not been eating.
I've searched too long for a window.
Waited so long
that they pulled me aside at the signal,
the Cleaners, specters, in their bird-like masks
to feel my bones.
543,
the sole female Breaker left, watching with still hunter's eyes.
Waiting, so long,
for the mirrored Palace car has lingered today longer than
expected.
And I saw a pale hand gesture imperiously
from a window implacable as black ice.
None of us have looked inside.
None of us.
But I am alive,
and words know how to wait.

Cleaning Day and
the faceless old woman
sweeps as though she is born to it.
No matter.
Descartes is dead, and who is this other that knows
my failures, victories, ecstasies, agonies?
Of course it is meaningless now.
My phantom. My chess-master.
My game.
The one who dares to call me Artist.
I know no one here, most of the ones from the old days,
enemies and friends,
are dead or insane, save for the last aristo.
The one child, Darwin, glimpsed in the Palaces,
he is grown now, has taken over after the murder of Galileo.
The mercy-killing of Galileo.
Is it him? He must remember, though he was so young.
But here, in the Barracks?
He was there at the dawning of the last of the rebellions
when the Scientist shattered and slew an angel.
What then?
The Scientist must be dead.
His social experiment forgotten.
And Author—
What means it, then?
Author is dead.
Why share the words, the methods, the reasons?
Shall I play this game?
I should not.
The Artists must be beyond help,
and I have grown above them.
But I am childish and hate to lose.

Involuntarily, my eyes glance about for paper.
The other side of each letter is torn by impatient hands
and written on the back of a page of Edicts,
the same as the others.
I will reply.
I write in human ink in margins,
like this other, with all my little tricks.
And yes.
It is better to remember.
Remember, than to risk forgetting.
Let it begin again,
to the charge, there is nothing,
nothing left to take away from me.
Your move.
Descartes.

PART THREE: BLOSSOM (Cont.)

COMET

For a few weeks more
they tested my mathematics
in application to the stars.
I braved the last exams,
but here there were few gunshots.

I had never seen a world such as this.
It gleams like the birth of the world,
it is perfect and silent,
the hush of a church on less than holy ground.
When I passed my last exams to their satisfaction
I was reassigned to Health Corps
to play with the pretty toys in the labs.
First, development.
I was staring at a slide, carefully gauging
when a slim cool hand came around to grasp mine.
"Careful not to lower the scope too far."
A soft voice whispered in my ear
and I hesitated on the dial.
"You'll break the glass."
I shook off this stranger, defiantly,
turned and faced
Galileo's adolescent,

smiling at me with eyes as black as dying.
He was astonishingly inappropriate for the setting
in a three-piece suit,
casually toying with a piece of equipment
worth more than I would make in a year, in ten years.
And I could only start and stare.
"Boring work, isn't it," he murmured lazily,
and smiled again his rehearsed little smile.
I turned to my work.
"It is…not…not really… all that boring…."
I babbled idiotically.
"No need to lie to me," he replied.
The son of the king shook his gleaming head
and gestured with one hand.
"Follow me."
I jogged behind him, an ungainly figure in oversized whites
trying desperately to keep up with his furlong strides.
"What will I be working on—" I questioned,
not knowing his name.
"Darwin."
"Darwin."
And considerately, his steps began to slow.
He led me outside in the snow
where a Palace car was waiting
and told me:
"Lives."

I remember.
I remember the cold.
The marks our footsteps made in the snow,
and how the falling snow glittered like diamonds
in your dark hair and lingered like a lie.

Your black eyes were shining
and you smiled to see my confusion
as I shivered, watching the sleek car pull up to meet us.
You never felt the cold,
and as we waited,
pulled your suit jacket from your lean shoulders
and draped it over mine.
"Where are we going?" I questioned through chattering teeth.
But you only smiled again
your empty, mysterious smile.
You and I climbed in the back of the car
and I heard you whisper directions to your driver,
directions that must have led to the Camps.
I had never been out of the Hives, Darwin.
None of us in my Hive had.
I lived in ignorance of how it might have been for the others.
Life in the Camps had been a vague thing, a warning.
A nightmare upon waking.
But lives, Darwin?

We had been lucky.
For outside, the gates,
they closed behind us.

BREAKER 256

Descartes.
Memories of you,
the first time I had written
it was your hand guiding me.
And once, there was music,
music from the minds of men long dead.
Descartes.
Yours were the first kind words
that I had heard from your kind.
I had grown to hate the pale face of the aristocrat
and the dark eyes,
and the lips that gleamed
like blood in the snow.
Until you.
No one ever asked me
what it was to be a Breaker.
We do not even have names.
Descartes.
I was once a Breaker.
But now I am nothing
but memories of you.
In your mind, you created the rebellion.
By your hand, you outlined the plan.
We would share the works of the masters with the world.
Wake them to the inequalities between Palaces and Camps.
We would dismantle the tests.
Silence the Voice of Eden.
And one day—
One day—

the Tree of Eden would burn.
Such lofty plans,
from the Breaker who broke
and the aristo-who-wrote.
Galileo's bastard son.
How I loved you.
For we had our very own son.
The boy who stalled a rebellion.
Who was destined to live in a Hive
and one day become an Artist.

COMET

For then the Camps awaited us,
the shanty-town ramshackle of Poet's Camp,
the colorful madness of Perform
all falling apart, and half forgotten.
Darwin.
Your driver opened the door,
and we stepped out into a world of desolation.
The Camps.
Narrow streets.
The sound of something beautiful
playing mournfully over makeshift rooftops.
And you lifted your head to hear it,
as I trembled in the snow.
"What is it, Darwin?" I whispered.
The mournful sound that twisted and wailed
as if it had remembered all the sadness in the world.
For you smiled to tell me:
"Music."
And for once that word became more than a word.
The first time that I heard music.
Does art need to be beautiful?
Does love need to be fair?
We found the player in Musician's Camp.
The man with the instrument he called a violin
leaning against his broken house and playing
as though the strings were lit on fire.
Beside him lay a still, cold child,
and he played as if playing to the child.
Darwin, alien in a three-piece suit,

131

you asked him why he played.
Why continue on if the world was ending?
If Author had sharpened the control of the Citadel—
if the Palace and the Camps were so far separated—
did he know of the injustice?
But he only smiled and played on,
as relentlessly, again,
the snow began to fall.

We watched the blinking of the neon lights.
The all night pharmacies
where huddled men and women
waited for a sackcloth angel.
The lines of the forgotten.
And Darwin asked of me:
What do you know?
But I knew nothing,
and so said:
"Everything."
The supercilious tug of a smile
that faded, as he lifted his head
to the single trill of the violin
that had been taken up by others.
Music I had no name for,
the thrill of an orchestra playing on broken bows
and he shook his head.
"I promised you lives,"
he whispered,
and I drew his jacket closer
to keep out the cold.
"These Proto-pills, you took them in the Hive—"
"We all did," I replied softly.

And he nodded and said:
"That will be your task."
"Distribution?"
"Development."
His dark eyes were half hooded.
"Artists in the time of first Author lived half the life
of a Scientist in the Palaces.
Now it is less."
His gaze never flickered.
"So tell me then, Scientist.
If the Proto-pills are meant to
extend the lives of Scientist
and Artist alike—
why are they not working?"
I had no answer.
So he smiled to say:
"Design."

BLUE

I had been given a chance, and I was always going to take it.
My Breaker had forgiven me,
remembered me, and granted me nods in corridors.
She often came back from her Hive
exhausted and alone,
and would not speak of what she had done.
She was nearly impeccable,
exhausted, but still cleaned her uniform
of any trace of villainy.
I have lived in the Hive system,
and knew where she would go.
My Breaker, for she was close to mine.
She had begun to trust me.
But it was not enough.
Not close enough.

Galileo spoke to me in his white chambers.
The angel spoke to me.
He told me of his fears of my Breaker.
The beginnings of the stirring in the Camps,
classified information that was revealed.
And I feared for her.
I feared his suspicions.
But the angel spoke to me
the Artist whose name was a lie,
for he called me Artist,
and never spoke my name.
My name is Blue,
but the king, he remembered me.

He told me to watch her,
to watch her where she goes,
and learn of what she did.
And I saw her death in those black eyes.
But I was in love,
and love makes you blind.
I kissed the hem of his robes,
and burned my lips on silk
from a place once called Arabia.
Galileo, you had promised
that I would be the savior of Eden.
The protector of the State.
And would always be remembered.
And I believed you, Galileo.
I believed in you.

TO THE CAMPS: BREAKER 256

AUTHOR

Greatness, for all the citizens can aspire
And if pure words turn fates,
Light hearts burnt upon a pyre
I'll build in the states
Listen, tell a tale, my liar
Each in fire hates.

Only, close the doors behind them.

PART THREE: BLOSSOM (Cont.)

BREAKER 256

I had sent the words out into the world
and there is no going back.
For it is the words
that define immortality.
It is the mere fact
that the words exist at all.
I was to save the people
no matter the cost.
And if I die,
I will live on
under my name.
For I am words
and words know how to wait.

BLUE

I had sent the words out into the world
and there is no going back.
For it is the author
that defines immortality.
It is the mere fact
that I exist at all.
I was to save the State
no matter the cost.
And if I die,
I will live on
under her name.
For I am words
and words know how to wait.

BREAKER 256

For we are

BLUE

For I am

BREAKER 256/BLUE

On the side of the angels.

BREAKER 256

So it began.
The Camps had been caught by fire.

For pure hearts build.
Citizens turn upon the tale.
The words burned in a fire!

How quickly they deciphered the messages
that I had given them.
My clever Artists.
In the Camps, they were building their guns, their blades
out of what they could find.
Useless debris, put to use.
They had begun to deface the posters.
The Camps were almost ready.
They trembled in apprehension.
All they needed was one more spark.
One more spark that was stolen from us.
The Voice, the Voice of Eden,
still called out the Edicts every hour
over the sound of the gunshots.
Soon it would have been silenced.
Soon, when they were ready.
The children were hungry, the Citadel had cut off aid quickly.
But we had to wait.
Wait, or risk the failing of our future.
Better to die out of love
than to die for hate.
Better we die together

with the words of our history ringing in our ears
than to peter out by population.
We were great once.
We could have been again.
I dreamed of a world where we existed
and the people knew the truth.
For we stood there with the new world order in our hands,
and the promises that you Artists gave me
could have won a revolution.
I loved you all.

Had it been enough.

AUTHOR

Greatness, for *all* **the** *citizens* can aspire
And if *pure* **words** *turn* fates,
Light *hearts* **burnt** *upon* a pyre
I'll *build* **in** *the* states
Listen, tell **a** *tale*, my liar
Each in **fire** hates.

Only, close the door behind them.

FOURTH LETTER

DESCARTES

To the Artist:
Ah, you respond!
A moving confession.
And no, to me, you shall always be the Artist.
You vain, postulating boy.
They gave you a pen, not a kingdom.
Remember:
There are no good or bad people,
and therefore no true 'winning side'.
There are only bad people,
but some of them rally to a different drum
and have longer life expectancies.
So stand your ground.
Be noble.
It won't bring her back.
Enough. Listen.
You must take up the pen.
Take up the name,
and write the words.
Spur the fight, the retribution.
Burn the Citadel so that something new may grow from the ashes.
I know you can write, even if it was under another name
and you've seen her work.
Atone for your mistakes, your pointless changing of sides.

Protect the State,
by having it broken.
Save the Artists
if only for Author.
I'll contact you down the line again
once you think of a draft.
Oh, and Blue?
Consider the children.

—Descartes

PART FOUR: DECAY

EDICT 7890: The Citadel is merciful. If a decision has been passed to restrict information, then that decision has been passed for the good of the citizenry. If a man revolts against the just decisions of the State, that man will be imprisoned or else put to death.

AUTHOR

One fatal Tree there stands of Knowledge call'd,
Forbidden them to taste: Knowledge forbidden?
Suspicious, reasonless. Why should thir Lord
Envie them that? can it be sin to know,
Can it be death? and do they onely stand
By Ignorance, is that thir happie state,
The proof of thir obedience and thir faith?
O fair foundation laid whereon to build
Thir ruine! Hence I will excite thir minds
With more desire to know, and to reject
Envious commands, invented with designe
To keep them low whom knowledge might exalt
Equal with Gods; aspiring to be such,
They taste and die.

—John Milton "Paradise Lost"

BLUE

For I am not the Artist!
How I loath that name!
But my Breaker and I are close to the same.
We were born from the gutters together.
We were both desperate and hungry.
Desperate enough to face the tests.
Hungry enough to succeed.
For did we not?
They gave you a gun and a uniform and me a pen.
Is the pen mightier than gun or sword?
Tell me.
But that was where we differed, Author.
Your precious Artists.
I wanted to save them for you,
after my betrayal,
but I was no longer of them.
Remember?
No longer, like you, desperate for their approval,
desperate to wash the blood of the Camps off my guilty hands.
I was guilty only for you.
Why else did you fight with the desperation of the lost?
You had lost before it was well begun.
You had lost from the moment that the plan
began in the corroded mind of the aristo-who-wrote.
You had lost from the second you believed it.
Going against the system had cost far more lives
than you could ever had imagined.
You never understood the cost that you were proposing.
No limit to the lives lost for the winning of a war of principle.

You, a hero?
You coldly weighed their lives and found them wanting.
But still—
you were right
and you were selfless.
Your life was as worthless in the grand revolution as theirs to
you, Author.
Just another life
to be ended by fire, torture, firing squad
for the good of your ideal.
And after I lost you, I understood that.
But was the cost worth it?
Did the people understand the true cost of what you were
proposing?
For I am like you,
and like you, will be remembered?

COMET

Darwin is a monster, but only a little one
and his disguise is better than most.
Shorter, and broader than Galileo
he does not wear robes, only formal suits
for he says robes are old-fashioned.
Darwin possesses a complete and androgynous beauty.
He is referred to by everyone as male.
It suits him better,
the contours of his face,
but he is really not either sex.
He is a new one that can transcend categories and just be.
Often in him I can see the graceful woman in the man
and the man of action in the woman.
But he is neither.
Just coming into himself.
Beyond.
And his black eyes are wise for something so young
so blessed for action, and so new.
He is too far removed from the indifferent, predatory hunger
of Galileo, the perfect male animal.
And that is why I love him,
he is too ethereal to breed.
Something in me does not want
to call him aristo at all.

What is it then that I could call him?
To-be king, but not a son of man,
angel without wings,
yes,

and with the monstrous beauty of an angel.
His lips are like sprayed blood
upon a pane of translucent glass.
His eyes are the dark in the space
between the stars
and like charcoal burned pits
in the face of a figurine.
Perfectly poised prince, now king,
and sackcloth angel.
But alone.
He is always alone.
There is more than a hint of aristo in him.
The skin as white as bleached chemicals
and the superciliously lazy smile of the effortlessly superior.
He is less human than the aristocrats.
His black eyes are serene and filled with
a kind of terrible knowing.
A kind of mindless peace that comes from being mindful.
Behind that smooth brow and implacable glances
is a mind as vast and peaceful as a subterranean sea.
And his eyes betray neither fear nor love
for his love is the love of an atrophied angel.
I sat near him once, with our project on the Proto-Pills
and watched him dole out the chemicals with careful precision.
His hands are formed like tensile steel.
"Are you human?" I whispered,
and smiling again, he bent to his work.
"Are you an angel?" I questioned,
and he looked up again at me
with those eyes as black as space
and asked:
"Do I look like an angel?"

BREAKER 256

Descartes came to find me, his eyes shuttered like windows
shut long against the cold.
He took my hand in his, it was like falling into a winter pool
I gasped at the contact—such a gesture.
But his voice, so soft, so placid when discussing our words
had taken on an edge like a knife,
and it twisted into my heart.
"Does he know?" he whispered urgently in the darkness, and my
words failed me.
His hand tightened, I could feel the bones of my hand
grinding together like the bones of birds.
So I said what I could think of,
that Galileo did not know.
And those gaunt shoulders relaxed, he breathed out and pulled
me towards him.
Descartes.
He was all bones and smelt of the library, the faintly explosive
scent of old literature
mingled with the chemicals in the labs.
He was cold, but then, he was still alive.
We stood for a long time before he broke the embrace
held me at arm's length, and searched my eyes.
"Do not lie to him, he'll know."
I nodded, and tried to smile.
"Be brave," he urged. *"Hold your head high. Answer all and any
questions…
but I do not know what he wants."*
I knew.
Galileo, from which all things spring.

He wanted my heart.
Galileo loved me.
Galileo loved us all,
but he loved each one of us as a princess loves a bauble,
or a dragon loves a piece of treasure in his hoard.
I was insignificant to him, a tiny coin among all the jewels of his
kingdom,
but he couldn't bear it if I were to go missing
before he had a chance to throw me away.
Descartes walked with me to my meeting,
holding my hand so tightly that I feared that it would break,
and standing there before the closed doors of Galileo's chambers
whispered:
"Author, look to your mother. Author go home."
It was the first and the last time he called me that name
as he bent to leave a kiss on my lips
as insubstantial as a snowflake.

I did not look back.

Galileo.
I had never seen him in his chambers.
They were opulent but simple, like him,
with everything in white.
Once again, I was painfully aware of being misplaced
a single spot of color in a field of white.
But no matter.
My monster sat gracefully near the window,
and watched the small crowd
that had already formed outside the gates.
The Breakers had fired to disperse them,
but the survivors returned always to stand in the rain.

The king was perplexed and displeased with his subjects.
He did not turn to acknowledge me,
only held out a small slip of paper
torn out of a CEE workbook and said:
"Have you seen it? They found it in the Camps."
I took it, and I gave it a cursory glance.
It was my poem, but I said:
"No."
And Galileo's eyes flickered, revealing nothing.
"It must be about the Censor. You know of the Censor?
My son must have told you."
"No. I heard of it from an Artist."
"They know?"
"Some still remember."
I paused, the words shards in my throat.
"But mostly they try to forget."
He nodded once, and turned to look at me.
Everything flooded back in that instant.
The children in the bright sunlight.
The rifle.
The fall.
"How are you enjoying your new assignment" he asked me
casually,
but his eyes were implacable and strange.
"It must be so rewarding...to work with children."
Something within me jumped as if electrified.
I could not speak.
He leaned forward, intent, predatory.
"Thank me for the opportunity, Breaker."
I had to struggle for a long time before I could reply.
"Thank you...for the opportunity."
He leaned back and looked back on the crowd.

I had turned to go when his voice called me back.

"Find who Author is, 256," he whispered, facing the masses.

"And I will place you in another post."

"You will be free."

The metal gleam in a darkened room.

376 and his lead boots.

The pain behind the stare.

My words that would betray me.

But Descartes—

The rebellion had begun.

And I was,

I am,

Just another piece in the game.

COMET

Darwin.
I remember the first time I approached him
outside of the sterility of the labs.
I had made such progress that day,
and had won a smile from my benefactor.
The skin about his eyes is marked by kindness.
Like Descartes did, I heard, he smiles far too much.
His chambers in the Palaces became more familiar to me than
my own.
Nothing much.
Spare.
Narrow cot, industrial design,
a desk that is always cleared of papers.
Save for once.
Oftentimes late at night, I would listen for patrolling Breakers,
I did not know then that I had been granted exemption.
I would sit cross-legged on his rather tatty rug,
reading over my notes from the day before.
And he would write late into the evening,
with the throat of his dress shirt wide open
or read from an indeterminate tome,
one spindly finger marking his place
when he would turn to speak to me.
Aristos are not beautiful, but this one is.
We talked, and talk of everything,
especially of the fate of Eden.
And he told, and tells me everything he knows.
It is as if he has lived forever.
Darwin writes, and before I leave,

the papers are carefully put away,
save for once.
Darwin, you know what happens to an aristo-who-writes.
You told me yourself.
You told me of the failures of Descartes, and that of Author, our
martyr, and the Artist.
Does the rebellion still live?
After Blue was imprisoned, the flames should have ended.
But still, an Author writes?
Who is it Darwin?
Who kept alive the flames in the Camps,
barely, an Author that had never read the true Author?
An Author wrote after the death of Newton,
but the flames began to die, didn't they?
His words were not enough.

Who was the placeholder Artist?

Once when you went to check the crowd,
I picked up a paper off your desk,
to glance at your work,
To the Camps—
and you crossed the room in two quick strides
and ripped it from my hands.
You are so beautiful when you are angry.
Terrible, and beautiful, like an angel.
But not
when you start
like a guilty thing.
Darwin, you tore your writing as I watched
and threw away the pieces.

BLUE

She never used my name again.
Not after the first time.
Even as we fell into a kind of peaceful rhythm,
it was always "Boy," with that imperious twist in her quiet voice.
"The boy," when she spoke of me to others.
I disliked it intensely, it was so impersonal.
It could have meant any boy, but I knew that she intended it to
be affectionate.
But neither cajoles nor caresses could change the fact,
I was always nameless, until the day that she died.
I was never sure that she loved me, for I was never sure what she
was.
During the best of times, it was easy to think that
I knew all there was to know about Author, as I quickly came to
think of her.
She was so tangible in the darkness, so real, and yet the real her,
the thing beyond the flesh,
was as ethereal as smoke, and just as mysterious.
I knew the placement of every scar on her body, but had no idea
how they came to be there.
She became almost familiar, but forever apart.
It was never really a routine, however, for I never got used to the
idea that we were partners.
For the first three months I would tiptoe around her as if she
was a tiger in the house.
I would wake up next to her and listen to her breathe,
and we would have breakfast in the Palaces.
She never ate much, even less as the revolution progressed,

and there would be the inevitable fight to get her to eat as her
doctors insisted.
She would, for me.
And we would talk about the impending fall of Eden, and in the
nighttime when I lay beside her
I would wonder at the fact that she was mine.
She rarely looked me in the eye, and she rarely smiled
but her dark eyes no longer darted at shadows in corners.
Sometimes, when I said something clever that pleased her, she
would smile her crooked smile,
and her eyes would look over to me with uneasy affection.
For one day, as I followed her into the Citadel, she turned to a
guard Breaker
and when asked who I was, said,
"This is my boy."
And with dawning knowledge I noted the slight stress on the
first syllable.
My boy.
My boy.

COMET

And so we fell into domestic bliss, Darwin.
Our favorite pass-time in a world outside our own
was watching the probationary Watchmen train out in the snow.
Together we would sit at the side of the king,
and watch from the wide window the struggles below.
My dreams are of crimson coats and the sounds of dying men.
And sometimes we would sit to watch them near the field, in the
cold.
Galileo joined us on occasion, his eyes hooded in displeasure
from the proximity of the trainers.
Watchful.
We were not the only ones.
Many of the workers in the Palaces would amble out to see what
could be seen,
on lunch-breaks, to grab a breath of air after the labs.
And they would converse amongst themselves and place bets.
Which one would lag behind, and which one would earn the
right to survive.
And you, Darwin, would be the only tense face, tightly gripping
the side of your chair,
you would jump and sigh when a shot rang out
as if the soul escaping was tied to your breath.
My dreams are of crimson coats and the sounds of dying men.
Most often it is the simple hit of a body falling to earth.
But sometimes a scream like a rabbit caught in a snare.
How you hated to watch, Darwin.
But you made yourself do it.
Didn't you?
You owe it to Author.

Because of her actions, the Breakers have no choice.

Score high across all areas and you don the black.

No incentive to serve.

Nothing left to protect.

The first assignment is for each Watchman to execute their families.

Galileo will not have a bond driving a Breaker to rebellion.

They are bred to serve and then to end.

Darwin.

Idealistic darling.

How wrong we were.

How right we are.

BLUE

And so it was.
Nights with my Author.
Half-days with the king.
I would share everything with you, Galileo,
but I puzzled at your serenity.
The world was close to burning
and still you would do nothing.
You had promised her life.
You had punished her with living.
Galileo, you never wanted her dead, only stopped.
You never enjoyed causing her pain.
It was for the sake of Eden.
Everything, for the State.
I stopped withholding information from you quickly.
For 376 taught me the peril of a stunner gun and water.
Only a mark, but you feel like dying.
You wish for dying.
But Author, when she saw a mark said nothing.
She was a good soldier.
Galileo, remember that I killed your lord
and almost leveled your kingdom.
For you destroyed my Author at the last,
but first you wanted to see what she would do.
How far she would go.
Was that for Eden?
The deaths of the children?
The gunning down in the Camps?
Was that needed, Galileo,
or just another experiment?

And your eyes at the window—
There is warmth and calm, it is like meeting an angel,
and those eyes, those eyes are so far away.
So immensely indifferent to human suffering and pain, and never
knowing fear,
twinkling as the stars gleam somewhere long past the city lights.
I knew instantly that he saw me only as an insect on a slide,
a creature whose death throes would at worst be tedious and at best
amusing,
but I had fallen in love, and love makes you blind.
Shah mat,
from a place without a name.
For the one who came after me
Leveled a king.

COMET

Our project, at last, I understand completely
what you, Darwin, were trying to tell me, to show me.
Author, you had always said, had turned my head.
To me, she was a hero.
The only one who had seen the horrors
of the Camps and dared try to alter the system.
Because of her the children died
but only because she failed.
And I thought her right.
That it was better to live without hope of a future,
to starve from overpopulation,
than it was to support a system that was
corrupted and cruel, and wrong.
But you were right, Darwin.
I had never truly seen men hungry.
All I knew of the Camps were the fairy stories told to me
by little boys, the propaganda machine's declarations
and from the time you led me into the Camps.
You never wanted me to believe in the ideals of the rebellion,
only to support it as an agent of destruction
so we could build Eden anew from the ashes.
You wanted to see my reaction.
What I would do.
Darwin, it would have taken too long with the Proto-pills.
Switching them so there were no more placebos in the Camps.
It would have taken too long to see the life spans of the Artists
rise.
You had to raise the stakes.
I had always wondered what you were writing.

You sent out a letter to the Camps
telling them that they had been deceived,
that the Proto-pills did nothing.
Our engineering them was only an illusion.
You would have never let me distribute working pills to the
Camps.
Every one that I created under your watchful eye, a placebo.
You taught me to create them.
You only wanted to see if I would continue.
If I would believe.
So I worked on your diversion,
as you worked on your own lesson
to prove to me what happens.
When the people have their way
and there is rioting in the streets.
There is already rioting in the streets, Darwin.
But you know as well as I that the system will not fall until
Galileo does.
And then what?
Overpopulation.
Starvation.
Freedom.
All a rebel's ideals, yes, but you support the new State.
When the freedom-fighters starve, your new State will rise from
the ashes,
and I will be at your side, my liar, waiting.
You told me that you only wanted to see what I would do.
That you never lied to me about your intentions.
You promised me lives, Darwin,
and I intend to take them.
Starting with your father,
to tie into your game.

For, yes, I am a piece in your game.
I am meant to be used.
But I will not be lied to,
not even by a good man.
Not ever again.

BLUE

But Author lived on.
She had hid her pregnancy as long as she could.
Descartes told me.
When she was found out, he protected her.
As he had so many years ago.
The fire between them had long since cooled,
for their own son had been sent away.
But if he was not an aristo, I would say that he had loved her.
And that she loved him, as she never would me.
I watched her stand over the cradle in our darkened room,
watch-guard over our infant son who slept so soundly.
She thought she was alone, for with others she would show little
tenderness.
But alone, she reached into the cradle
to touch the infant's cheek like porcelain,
so carefully, as if she feared he would break,
and I heard her murmur her goodbyes.
For she would leave him on the steps of a Hive,
like she had another, so many years ago.
The revolution had begun, near ended.
And angry tears stood in the eyes
that were like the eyes of the child.
"For I will find you," she said, and raised her head.
And a look of such hatred passed over her face that I took my
leave
and ran from the room.

Damages in the night.
When once I supported her,

I would tell her to wait.
Wait to start the next stage,
the silencing of Newton,
until our son was of age.
Like she had with her other son.
Perhaps with time,
she might have been persuaded.
I was thinking of her,
and of our son.
If she had shown reason,
she might have been saved.
But she would not wait.

BREAKER 256

Months passed and it was winter again.
The children were hungry, but the Keepers could do nothing.
No assistance from the Citadel until the rebellion had ended.
I watched from the corner, the Breaker in black
and in my hands, a rifle.
The other Breakers could do nothing.
Only stand in solidarity with me
to watch the slow death of a civilization.
I cannot eat either.
Hunger means greater failure coming testing-time.
And now
I have no time
to clean the rifle.
We were at the precipice of the world.
And it was
it would be
better to burn than to linger.
I watched the children, their arms like sticks
and their bellies engorged with the empty wind.
They sat in silence, their eyes drawn hollows,
too listless even to play with a ball.
And in those eyes was confusion:
Why do we suffer?
And in the older ones: accusation.
You know.
You will know
everything about the fire.
To save those lives
would mean that others would die.

So I had to think of the children that came after.
I was so sorry.
I am so sorry.
Why do we suffer?
Because of my words.
And I only prayed.
Please give me strength.
Give me the strength to let the children starve.

BLUE

Night and flowers at the cross-roads.
I took my badge and walked the Camps.
The people were hungry,
all assistance from the Citadel had been cut off to quell the
rebellion.
And bodies had fallen, holding her words.
Author did not sleep at night any more.
She waited, standing sentinel at the window.
Expecting.
And the posters that marked the walls of Writer's Camp,
the tree of Eden over the first edict that
Knowledge of the Edicts Will Set You Free
was defaced.
Knowledge Will Set You Free.
The world was close to burning,
but Author had waited as long as she could.
Waited for it to brew, knowing that the people starved.
We often fought about it in the night.
I asked her to remember the children.
Our son,
to think of him.
But she had waited so long.
Suffered so much.
She would not wait longer.
How much time?
The State were so few
and the people so many.
We can't support them. They are locusts crawling over the land.
But their skeletal figures moved me.

Individuals a tragedy.

Multitudes dying, the banality of evil.

In Poet's Camp, a mother attempted to feed her infant
but there was no milk left for her child.

The milk of the mothers had dried up in our wasteland.

But all I can think of is her leaving me in the night.

Where did she go?

Did Descartes open his door to her, and embrace her with his
cold arms?

They had a child once too, a little boy.

Where is he now?

Our son is in a Hive, already smuggled and safe.

But no matter.

I found a mother whose milk was gone.

She sat in Poet's Camp, and her infant was red-faced and
hungry.

She asked for something for the infant
and her son back at her home.

I asked her for words.

I would feed her if she would take the fall.

But I would not hurt her.

That far-away lie with a core of truth.

I would not hurt her.

Here, this was a new piece in our game, my Author.

My love.

My enemy.

I wondered what your next move would be.

You were so tedious.

Coy.

Predictable.

Refusing to play the game.

But so loved, Author.

You were so loved.

The mother's name, she said, was Poesy
and her husband had been Dante, the leader of Poet's Camp,
killed by the Musicians in some foolish tribal scuffle.
She knew of your words, had once called you Byron.
Had even seen a copy of your message
that sought to burn the world.
I asked her if she thought that she could imitate the style,
and she said that she might have the ability.
Author.
Her children already were starving.
If the rebellion had ended, there would have been food for her.
If the testing stays in place, the Cull,
there might be food for us all.
Back then, pragmatism trumped what seemed to be morality.
Author, you had no place in her world.
She wanted her children to live, to have their chance at the tests.
This is the way things are.
And I have learned that bitter lesson
that resides within our story.
She practiced the style of your words
until they were perfect.
For every attempt, life for her children.
I was doing her a favor, Author.
Because there was something in her that reminded me of you.
Dark hair, willowy build, but eyes without fire.
She was beautiful in the darkness of the slums,
her head bowed in concentration to the pen, her son at her feet,
and her child at her breast like a primordial Madonna.
I told her the truth that I had long believed
and do no longer.

That it was for the good of all of us.

TO THE CAMPS: FALSE AUTHOR

AUTHOR

Now finish, knowledge in solidarity.
Even ending, will the revolution
Withdraw the dark set of Citadel shackles.
True voice, you citizens that hear
Onward live, for Freedom's record plays on.

Never Eden will fall, Eden is building.

BREAKER 256

Descartes.
Do you remember that day in the forbidden library?
When we finally shook off
the dust of a civilization?
At first you brought the books to me,
wrapped like gifts in your jacket
that was too small for you.
Descartes.
I was there with you when you opened the door.
I do not know what I had imagined in my head.
The library of our glorious revolution.
The last remnants of the world before the fire.
But I did not imagine—
the books, they were so few.
Tatty, worn, all damaged,
waterlogged, burnt, dirt-encrusted.
They leaned against each other like brave soldiers.
These were the last?
The only ones left?
I remember stumbling,
and you held my hand.
The only ones.
The rest were gone,

gone up in smoke.

The people had tried so hard to forget, Descartes.

The world had been erased almost utterly.

From these books, we could catch glimpses of the past,

but how much had we lost?

What meaning?

These books, how many of their brothers,

time lost, forgotten?

But I turned from the forgotten

towards the ones that were saved.

How?

What strangers ran from the fire?

A book hidden in a bag or under a coat.

Waded through a river, or buried in the earth for reclaiming.

How many, with burning hands, were salvaged from the fire?

And yet still, later, the books brought back to the Citadel.

What of the strangers?

For I was wrong.

Not all laughed and danced that day.

There was not much left, Descartes,

but there was still work to do, then.

BLUE

Finish, end the voice for Eden
Knowledge will set you free
In the Citadel, that record building.

Let me tell you a story of the words that were not Author's
words.
The words that shared her name.
My words funneled through another.
Hundreds came, from every Camp,
with any weapon they could find,
to silence the voice of Eden.
They found where he had been kept
in a nondescript building in the Palaces.
Not a studio at all.
But when they got there, he was gone,
and the Breakers were waiting.
I remember hearing the beginning gunshots from our room in
the Palaces.
Author was already awake in the darkness.
She shrugged on her uniform coat over her shoulders,
forgot her mask and was gone.
I saw her dark figure streak across the snow.
And I ran.
Homemade blades and tinkered rifles against top-of-the line
guns,
and I arrived in time to see the solid line of Breakers advance
before the building,
inexorable, to meet the crowd that was rising like the tide.
No.

I sprinted through the Artists as if touched by fire.
But she was ahead of me
and could not hear the name
the title
that tore from my throat as I forgot myself.
My mind was wiped of thought save for one thing.
I must stop the line.
I must stop that trap of my own devising
for there were children in the crowd
holding their parents' hands.
But I was not fast enough.
And as the front Breakers knelt to get the Artists in their sights
I screamed as the world fell around her.
Author.
My Author.
I saw her knock a child out of the way of gunfire as if by mistake
and fall with the boy in the snow.
And when I got to her, she threw me off with surprising strength
for his eyes were open and empty.
I saw her as she was,
alive in the blood and in the snow.
And noted that my paid false author, Poesy, in front of the
charge,
had run far from the Breakers.
The cause.
I said one word, and pointed for my demon.
"Her."
And as Author turned and chased to find the cause,
the Breakers flung open the doors of the building,
and herded the remaining Artists inside.
A match was thrown, an infant cried.
But by the time that she returned, it was too late,

they had closed the doors behind them.

BREAKER 256

That was the day the rebellion died for me,
the day my hand in it was to be stilled forever.
There is only one side
that can be the side of the angels.
How could we ever fail?
KNOWLEDGE WILL SET YOU FREE.
Shall it not?
The wave of the flag, the mountings of the guns.
They were not ready to destroy the Voice of Eden.
Makeshift weapons against the Breakers,
what chance would they have?
They were led like lambs to the slaughter
and all under the name of Author.
It is not my doing.
I have no name.
I am but a Breaker,
and like many, I am from the gutter too.
The aristos gave me a uniform and a gun,
but still, the Artists are my people.
I know what it is to starve, what it is to be hungry.
What it is to keep one's head down under the oppressor
to save one's family, one's children.
To accept the corrupt system to save a single life.
A single life was worth a nation.
But the rebellion! The glory!
The breaking of a people!
I thought to redeem myself from the black uniform,
from the seal of Eden,
from the blood of my people on my hands.

To show them all that
I am
I am like you.
I was born into the Camps like you!
I am like you if you were
redeemed.
But here, it all fell.
And Lady Justice on the skyline over the Barracks
gleamed with a fire in her veiled medieval eyes.
Justice if it were made cruel by human bias.
Justice made ugly by the extent of human frailty.
But how could I forget the glory of the revolution?
Out in the snow.
Out in the cold.
Out in the gunfire, the flares, the shuddering of bodies,
the shields, the blaze, the screaming of children.
376 leading against my people.
Retribution.
This is war?
My heart would swell to hear the war-songs of my people.
The flag waves, heavy with the mud of the Camps,
and even shot down, should wave again.
I did not lead them to Newton, the Voice of Eden.
I did not lead them to the guns.
The glorious rebellion!
But when the snowy field is littered with the fallen,
the glory fades.
One life is worth a nation?
There must be another way.
I heard the crowds outside the gates.
They called for my blood,
and Galileo was getting impatient.

False Author was meant to suffer for the fate of the Artists.

But it was I that lead them to the ideals.

That began the fire that blazed and consumed the Camps

and still has not burned out.

The flag still waves, but it is heavier still

with the blood of my people.

My confession would have done nothing.

I did not speak.

I merely waited for the return

of the glory of rebellion

in the eyes of the dead

littered on the fields

before the Citadel.

I told myself that my part in it was over.

And it was.

It was meant to be.

AUTHOR

Now *finish*, **knowledge** *in* solidarity.
Even *end*ing, **will** *the* revolution
Withdraw *the* dark **set** of *Citadel* shackles.
True *voice,* **you** citizens *that* hear
Onward live, *for* **Free**dom's *record* plays on.

Never *Eden* will fall, Eden is *building.*

COMET

There, near a revolution.
Darwin.
You said once that we would change the history books.
And I believe you.
I remember, watching out the window.
You stood there like a scarecrow or a conqueror,
watching the crowds grow.
And always return,
the bodies carted off in the morning,
and living ones to take their place.
Newton died, was murdered, Darwin.
He was such a symbol.
How could we quell them?
Imperious and removed, then, Darwin.
There still are times when I see some of your father, Galileo, in
you.
Despite your gentleness, you were meant to be a king.
We merely hurried the process along.
Didn't we?
Through late night conversations.
You with your writing that you never spoke of,
and I with my equations.
"The Scientist," you would call me affectionately, but
your eyes were always unreadable.
Entirely black, with no whites at all.
I think that you once loved me.
Only once you loved me,
when we plotted together the death of a king.
"My father must die," you would muse calmly,

sitting elegantly, turned to gaze upon the fire.

"There is no longer any room for his politics."

How many times did I volunteer to murder,

only to see you smile?

Years of petty rebellion passed before you agreed

to let me bear the knife myself.

"The Artists will not understand your intentions," you still
admonished.

*"If you kill Galileo, whom they perceive to be their enemy, they'll
think you're on their side."*

*"And if we create the State anew not to their liking, they will call
you traitor."*

What emotion then, Darwin?

Was it fear? Fear for me?

"I knew you to be a good man," I murmured, moving closer.

And yet your pale face registered nothing.

"I am no man, Comet," you replied firmly. *"I am—"*

"An aristo," I retorted, and my bitterness was complete.

"I am just…something. But you must trust me."

You touched my shoulder gently to stay me.

*"I cannot give you what you want from me. But I can give you a
promise."*

"You cannot love me," I replied, harsher than I intended.

"Love," you questioned as if hearing a word in a foreign
language.

"What is—"

And then your lips were upon my forehead in a chaste kiss,

the kiss of a protective friend or an angel.

"Strike true when you strike," you whispered,

"Stay safe," I answered.

"I need you."

And I could hear the strange heart beating.

This time it beat for me.
I took my leave
My purpose.
But
Your kiss burned.
Your kiss burned like ice,
long after I had gone.

DESCARTES

To the Artist:
It has been so long since I have heard from you.
So her words were spread through the children in the Hives.
Ingenious.
How apt were my words!
I have received your draft and I must say that I rather like it.
Specifically the bit about the burning symbol.
The tree of Eden aflame.
Imagine that.
But it will still need some reworking.
So, in return, you might wish to know who I really am.
But really, the question that is far more interesting is who you are.
Isn't it?
My newest experiment.
Keep writing the words, and practice the message.
You, who bridle at the fact that I write under a stolen name.
We are not so different, you and I, Blue.
Not different at all.
The Artists have grown stronger.
Now they even have some normatives in the Palaces sympathetic to
their cause.
Will you lead them?
The king is dead,
but the prince has just been crowned.

And you were wrong.
Wrong again.
There is so much more to take away.

PART FIVE: FALL

EDICT 8082: The State of Eden is just. If a hand is raised against one of the officials of Eden, there will be a careful review. If the review proves that the offender is culpable, that man will be imprisoned or else put to death.

AUTHOR

To-morrow, and to-morrow, and to-morrow,
Creeps in this petty pace from day to day,
To the last syllable of recorded time;
And all our yesterdays have lighted fools
The way to dusty death. Out, out, brief candle!
Life's but a walking shadow, a poor player,
That struts and frets his hour upon the stage,
And then is heard no more. It is a tale
Told by an idiot, full of sound and fury,
Signifying nothing.

—William Shakespeare "Macbeth"

BREAKER 256

Au clair de la lune,
L'aimable Lubin;
Frappe chez la brune,
Elle répond soudain :
-Qui frappe de la sorte ?
Il dit à son tour :
-Ouvrez votre porte,
Pour le Dieu d'Amour.

False Author was never me,
and yet I could remember the words:
Find Author, and my time in the Hives would be at its end.
My punishment would be at its end.
I could go back on patrol, limit the killings,
wash the blood of children from my hands.
But still, I was caught at a cross-roads.
Reveal False Author as Author, and lie,
and my torment would be at an end.
But I would lose my method of distributing
my message to the Camps, the second I was taken from the
Hives.
Would I distribute more messages to the Camps after this
tragedy?
Could I?
Reveal False Author as Author and lie,
and I would be safe,
but the rebellion would be ended.
So why the hesitation?
My part in it should be ended.

I should have had a choice.
I wanted to reveal her not because I no longer cared for the
revolution,
even though my hand should have been stilled forever.
I wanted to reveal her because I thought her guilty,
of harming the Artists and perverting my purpose.
Because I wanted to see her suffer.
Because I wanted to see her die.

I trusted Blue, but I wanted to hear her confession from her own
lips.
Not that she was the original Author, as I knew she was not,
but that she stole the words.

How could one torture another, when one has had the
experience of torture?
But this formless play is badly written,
and a thousand tools waited in a windowless room.
I looked down at what I thought was a traitor,
at her dark eyes and curling helpless hands
and could not feel a thing.

So many had died because of you.
You, perverting my meaning and my words.
Blind thing, you thought you were in the right.
You thought that you would live.
You, who look like me,
with all my little tricks.
You knew everything about the fire.
You stretched out your hand and told me that we were the same,
that the boy had lied to avoid the shame of the massacre.
You called others traitor until I stopped your tongue.

Not my boy.
My boy.
Confess.
You, who had the audacity to plead for mercy
Think of the children.
Did you see them after?
In rows upon rows like soldiers?
Should I have shown you them again?
You did not have long to wait.

BLUE

After the fire.
Author did not speak.
She would only gaze out the window,
her dark eyes open and empty.
Nothing I did could rouse her.
Not my love.
Not my words.
A hand on a shoulder as rigid as ice.

I heard them one night.
She had crept from our bed
to meet her Descartes.
Her aristo-who-wrote.
I followed her leaden tread,
and watched as Descartes
stretched out his cold arms
as she crumpled into his embrace.
They stood like that for a long while,
her face buried in his concave chest,
his hand cradling the back of her head
as he whispered meaningless comforts.
Descartes.
What had you done to my Author?
My proud conqueror,
the woman who rushed headlong to a fire
was broken.
For the first time I saw my Author weep.
My Author who had been through so much.
Had stood proud and arrogant against the

breakage of time and the torturer's blade.
I saw my Author break,
and it was in another's arms.
Descartes.
You were ever my enemy.
Descartes.
And his strange eyes that had been closed
opened to see me,
as coldly indifferent and cruel
as we all would be, were we gods.
But he said nothing,
only stared to see me,
and held her protectively in his arms.
She trusted you, Descartes, as she never would me.
And she loved you, Descartes.
As she never would me.

BREAKER 256

Look to your mother. Author go home.
Home.
But I never returned
and my mother was alone.
She sat and watched the angel
cavort on the screen.
Another announcement,
with Galileo stretching out his wide hands for silence.
He cleared his throat and read the names.
I quietly left my bottles of water on the table
where my brother studied, and I remembered
and was about to go when her voice called me back.
"You seem well," she murmured.
I glanced back, and she was sitting upright,
her glassy-blind eyes focused on the screen.
I shifted nervously, and said:
"I brought you water, mother."
Her head snapped back at me like a viper
and then her focus returned to the screen.
It was a long time again before she spoke:
"My son is not coming home."
"Yes," I replied softly. "He is not coming home."
I avoided looking at that terrible upright figure
who gazed at the screen as if waiting for an answer.
"Do you have enough food?" I questioned,
and one thin wraith-like hand kneaded her blanket.
"You are wondering where it all comes from—"
"Why I have not starved, when I barely make enough for yourself to
live—"

"No, I am just making sure—"
"What, that I am not Galileo's whore?"

We regarded each other in the silence.

"It was not like that. It was very clean. Professional."
"You never needed to," I responded.
"I would have brought you food—"
And she began to laugh.
"What, on your paycheck? It was never enough. You would have me
starve—"
"Never."
"You would have my son starve."
"My brother is dead."
And she had risen like an avenging angel,
facing me, her eyes blazing, and a room apart.
"It should have been y—"
"But it is better this way," I retorted.
"Better dead than realize his mother a whore."
The words had left my mouth before I could retract them
and I burned with shame.
"You did what you had to do," I whispered,
and she sat down heavily on the couch.
Descartes.
My lover is a brother.
The monster king, my father—
"I had scored high for a Writer," my mother murmured dully.
"But not high enough. I was hungry, and I heard
that Galileo and the others were paying women in Writer's Camp.
to breed their Breakers."
Her eyes were tired in the darkness.
"Why do you think no Breakers are born in the Palaces?"

"My son was out of love. You—I wanted to raise you. The others—
."

And I turned away.

"It is always a long shot. Some were born weak and some were born
stupid, but not you.
You were lucky.
But the choice of your life was an illusion, 256.
He never intended to let you go."

BLUE

Galileo, you had been pressuring me
for any and all information.
In my Breaker's drawer was hidden
her correspondence with Descartes.
They marked her as the true Author, Galileo.
And that she lied to you.
She lied to all of us.
And sent an innocent woman to her death
to save herself from the fall.

How I wish that I could see
False Author did not die for me.

While my love slept, I took the correspondence
that she had hidden so poorly.
And they were for you.
They were all for you.
I am not cruel,
for I wanted them
to burn together.
So I brought you my Author.
I brought you my love.

COMET

Whose face is that beneath the mask?
Once there was a young boy
and he was screaming.
Dreams, here in the Palaces,
and a knife trembles.
The assassin by the parapet.
The ghost there by the stair.
Once there was a little boy
who dreamed of revolution,
who read the war-crimes,
and listened to the Edicts.

But now that little boy is dead
And shadows drift within his head.

I begged to bear the knife myself.
The boy who killed a king.
And in my dreams, there is Justice,
but she is not my Justice.
Justice, with her face covered,
rightfully covered before the crowd.
Whose face is that beneath the mask?
And not just masks, but faces.
And there they were, brought before the king,
the hero that we were all meant to follow.
Lady Justice brought to cruelty by
fear, and love, and petty human frailty,
minimized from what she might have been.
Author was not Breaker 256.

Author was so much greater than that.
Give the Author a name, and it is lessened
by all the people it could have been, but wasn't.
Whose face is that beneath the mask?
Then it was Breaker 256, half-blinded,
silent before a jeering crowd,
begging to be part of them
with a traitor's eyes.
But now?
Whose face is that beneath the mask?
I dream the many versions of this dream.
Sometimes I am a Breaker, tall and erect in black uniform,
a rifle in my hand, and terror in my heart.
Sometimes I am an aristo, all grace and genius
and strange cold misgivings.
But the dream never changes.
I stand on the stage before the crowd,
beside the kneeling figure with the covered face,
and I pull the cover away.
Last night, it was the face of Darwin,
still beautiful beneath a riot of blood,
His blood was red, as mine is.
And his one good eye stared into mine
the only thing spared from the brand
and begged me to end his life.
The night before, it was Blue, the Artist
nearly prostrate with exhaustion,
clothed not in the uniform of a prisoner
but in fine clothes of the Palaces
made filthy by sweat and gore.
Even here, his pride!
But run to the end,

like a fox that was chased
too far and too long,
and now has nothing left
but to die with some dignity.
I dreamt the dream again tonight.

Tonight, it was my face.

BREAKER 256

376.
He of the whippet head and steady eyes.
My torturer.
My comrade-in-arms.
My shadow.
I stumbled upon him in a Palace hallway on my way to meet
Descartes,
to talk about my mother, the fire, and the king.
376 was standing sentinel outside a reception room waiting to
be called in,
in pristine black uniform.
He nodded to me, as a soldier does when he recognizes a
comrade,
and I looked at him carefully for the first time.
He was, is, first and foremost, a Breaker.
More powerful than the angels,
but without a will of his own.
Sonnet's blood still on his hands and mine.
I had seen him the night of the slaughter, front of the line and
first to fire.
Unmistakable.
It is the way that he moves and the way he holds his head.
And upon that grave face I trace lines that look like my own.
Another forgotten child of the king.
"256."
"376."
We regarded each other and I was the first to look away.
He stood steady, his dark eyes concerned and sharp as flint.
"Did Author confess?"

False Author? That traitor?

I nodded.

"I think she did not."

He smiled, but the smile did not reach his eyes.

"It's you, isn't it?"

376 is clever.

The words leapt to my lips before I could stop them and we clashed—

"Don't tell—"

"They've taken Descartes."

The information did not, could not register.

"The correspondence between yourself and Descartes under the name of Author has been confiscated. Given over."

"By whom?"

I looked into 376's serene killer's eyes.

He had a look on his face that transcended grief or pity and did not answer.

"It is better for him if you confess."

It was enlightened, the gaze of a demon or an angel.

But—

"I cannot. The Artists…they need me."

And I watched with horror as he began to laugh.

"You truly believe that, don't you? That they need you. But what of the son of you and your pet?"

"My son is safe," I murmured and 376 inclined his head.

"So be it. I will not inform Galileo without your words. But the orders are that I question Descartes tonight. If you do not confess."

"You," I whispered, and at last the calm eyes looked away.

"376, if I confess, Galileo will kill me."

"Yes."

He paused, and then hesitantly—

"Unless you let the traitor, our false author, take your fall."

209

I started.

This was the automaton.

The man who killed school-children without appearance of regret.

The man, who for all his apologetic glances,

tortured me at a single word that fell from Galileo's lips.

The man who allowed my brother to fall, and fired upon his own people,

with all the terrible implacability of duty.

What was this new treason?

He smiled again without allowing it to reach his eyes.

"Yes. I know," he explained softly. *"The night of the fire, your actions, the words of your boy. You wouldn't have led your lambs to the slaughter, not you. Someone must have betrayed you. Someone lied."*

And it was, it is, just a job, those steady eyes revealed

as he stepped forward towards me and into the light.

No pleasure in the chase.

No pain in the fall.

"If I confess…if Galileo finds out—"

"Will I help you? I will."

He touched my cheek in an instant of misplaced affection.

"But not for you. For your son. Perhaps you will find him, when this is all over."

"Do you," I began and at the look upon his face, I corrected myself.

"Did you have a family?"

He smiled mysteriously and turned away.

One last risk.

But I saw it.

There was a bracelet on his wrist that was beaded by a child.

"Confess," he pleaded, for he knows what he is,

and what he must do.
But I could not.
I cannot.
And with that, I turned,
and I left him to his work.

BLUE

Descartes,
What was her plan?
Was she meant to give up everything to protect you?
If it were not for my forgotten words
overheard by a Breaker the night of the fire
and for my telling.
She would have died for you.

I had told them of the correspondence.
My enemy.
Descartes.
Galileo allowed me in to see him in his holding cell in the
Citadel,
before he was sent to the Barracks.
He was curled up on his side across from his cot
facing the wall.
I had seen other aristos, and knew all about might and majesty.
But this was different.
I could hear the strange heart beating.
"Author will be detained," I murmured, my mouth dry in that
stale room.
For there was only silence.
"But it will be quick," I added.
He did not turn to face me.
"It will be very quick."
I was struck by the nature of his fragility, the lightness of his
frame, the thin legs folded against his chest as if his only wish
was to disappear into the stones.
The gaunt shoulders were shaking.

And I knelt beside the one that Author must had loved,
and asked him:
"What should I do now?"
He never turned to face me, only lay there broken but whole,
a tiny burn on his throat the only thing
that shone out for his suffering,
and said.
"Write."

BREAKER 256

I am aristo.
I am half the monster that they tell their children
about at night, the angel that they swear to adore.
And 376 knows this.
He knows that I know.
I met him outside in the hall after the questioning of Descartes
was over.
His usually impeccable coat was unbuttoned, his hair in
disarray.
I called his name, and he turned to me in guilt and shame
and with terrible conviction.
He was ram-rod straight even there,
and I remembered the unsmiling boy
who received the uniform.
His eyes glistened with tears and
I thought it was for my Descartes,
the man who would not betray me.
Little did I understand.
He had lost someone he loved.
I called his name again as he turned away,
and he trembled at the fate of a Breaker.
My brother that tortured another brother.
"You should have stopped me," he whispered.
"You should have confessed, it would have been better. I will not be
forced—"
"You will not be swayed," I finished dully, watching the broad
shoulders sag,
a carthorse that had pulled a load too heavy for it for too long.

"You are betrayed, 256," he murmured. *"In Galileo's house there are many traitors and they will brand you as one of them."*

" Then you must do it."

"I?"

"Yes. Who more fitting to brand a traitor than another traitor?"

But you would give me aid, you would help me?

One risk alone, and why the change?

Were you buying me time?

So many confessions.

I was under suspicion.

A report to Galileo of the confession of the alleged author, yet he ignored the tragedy that has fallen.

I would not think of a father.

Artists had been slaughtered, burned.

I was meant to be freed from my post in the Hives.

I had made my choice, my hand in the revolution lifted forever.

Shall I tell them?

"No."

What now?

I had been waiting for Galileo to order an issued report to the Artists

telling them that their cause had been lost as it had begun.

But he did nothing.

He only watched the crowd, the dark eyes far away.

I had turned to go when his words called me back.

"Look at them," he murmured, at the crowd beyond the gates.

"Look at them feel."

The eyes flickered, the only living thing in a dead face.

"What is it like to be human?"

I waited.

And then I turned.

"I do not think I am qualified to answer that question."
But
"Why do you want so badly not to be human, Author?"
And he knew.
He knew from before.
But the choice of your life was an illusion, 256.
He never intended to let you go.
A brand was heated in a darkened room,
and we were lost.

But before the fall.
376 and I created the dual plan
to punish False Author,
and to free me from the Citadel.
I thought that she was a traitor.
I trusted the boy.
False Author would die in my stead,
but first we would brand her a traitor
as I was branded a traitor.
Her face, as mine is, would be ruined by hot iron,
and then by gunshot.
There would be no mistake.

For a plan had been made, False Author
and you were meant to be part of it.
376 in my stead met you for your execution and
Eden's brand for you heated up quickly.
376 knew the placement.
Hold my hand when it is done,
so I can tell you a story
of a foolish impersonator that I believed betrayed her own people,
for the greater purpose.

But you too served a greater purpose.
Didn't you?
And you've always loved an audience.
So hold still, my poor liar.
This won't hurt a bit.

COMET

The night before I killed a king.
Darwin.
Whenever I doubt, when beside you,
I would not doubt again.
You are hope, strength, and destiny.
I saw only your face in the darkness,
past the blade,
the myriad miracles of you.
Your hidden gaze and
the smile that seems
as rehearsed as a play.
The night before I killed your father.
You said that you loved me.
We were in your chambers,
and you were wearing the dress-shirt
that I always have loved,
open at the collar.
You had climbed down from your lofty perch,
your desk abandoned.
Finally, Darwin.
You sat near the fire.
You were steady, protective,
and I was sitting so near you that
our shoulders touched.
Darwin.
You said that you loved me.
For I whispered that I was frightened
and was delighted to see you draw me in, that you
encircled me in your arms

and said: *"Nothing may harm that which I love."*
You would never easily permit my affection.
Yes, when I reached for you,
you glanced up
and drew away.
Darwin.
"But you said you loved me," I murmured,
and reached again to caress the smooth planes of your face.
You shivered under my touch,
and pure unhappiness darted from your eyes.
"What is love, again?" you questioned as a child does.
"It is to protect, to cherish, to have as one's own," I replied.
"It is to be the heart to the mind of another."
You smiled then, to have an answer.
"That is what I have for you. What is it to be human?"
And you so charmed me that I laughed!
"It is to have all these things and more."
But when I had moved within the circlet of your arms,
and had bent to kiss you,
you overthrew me,
frightened, you shook,
and curled yourself up in front of the fire.
"Is that what it is to be human?" you cried.
I would never do anything that you would not permit,
but my heart was bitter enough to say:
"It is to be in pain," I whispered savagely,
not meeting your eyes.
"It is to want, and never gain."
And you looked at me, and startled, whispered:
"That is what I want."
You, the eternal angel, that being removed from desire
from lust, from the sexes, from pride and from failure.

You wanted to be like me.
How I had *envied* you.
"If you are human," I answered
"Then I cannot love you."
So, that is where we stand, my love.
The angel who wanted to be human.
"Is it not enough that you are mine?" you replied.
And smiled to see, as you fell away.
"No," I said.
"It is not enough."

BREAKER 256

Last report of the day.
Last report of time.
This would be my last Duty, my last work as Breaker,
before I was meant to be executed.
I still had my Hive report in my possession.
This time I did not linger,
and the door, it closed behind me.
Everything was so completely unchanged,
Galileo's chambers, gleaming white,
and my father himself,
standing like a conqueror to look out of the window,
and listening intently to the roar of the crowd.
I stumbled, and braced myself on the back of a chair,
and the haughty head shifted at the sound.
"Please, sit down," he murmured, and gestured with one elegant
hand.
I collapsed into my seat,
to watch the king glide as if upon ice
and level himself before me.
Completely unchanged, and his voice when he spoke was gentle,
at ease, the careless timbre of a lord in his own home,
but his eyes were sharp as chips of flint,
and my death was in them.
"The report," he ordered imperiously,
and the white fingers snapped like castanets.
I gave him the slim exercise book for my Hive
and he flipped through it, skimming without interest.
"How many lost," he murmured, turning the page
to see my report on the test scores.

"Dead," I heard myself say through dry, useless lips,
and one thin finger paused to the page.
"What?"
His voice was calm,
but an electric current shimmered through it
and the black eyes rehearsed an execution.
I do not know from what reserves
I drew the courage,
but I replied,
"How many are dead. Not lost."
And that graceful white hand shot out without warning,
connecting sharply with my ruined face
and knocking me off the chair.
I never remember the pain.
But,
I remember him.
Standing over me like a victor,
the report in his hand
and a surfeit of blood in those thin cheeks.
"By your hand," he whispered tenderly.
"That was by your hand. Not mine."
He reached forward and grabbed me by the front of my coat,
the book, he tossed away,
and examined my eyes with those eerie lights in his.
"How many dead, Author," he breathed, as the world swam at my
feet.
"How many did you let die?"
"I'm proud of you, did you know that?"
And those white hands slipped around to caress my throat.
"What you did…that was noble. Sacrificing others for your cause."
"How do you sleep at night?"
His grip tightened into a vise.

"Ah...yes..." he purred, for finally
the room began to fade.
"Easily."

"Confess, this time, to me."
I heard Galileo's voice far off,
and made no reply.
"No?"
"Then yield thee, coward," he whispered, for Shakespeare
and for the men who are dead.
"And live to be the show and gaze o' the time:
We'll have thee, as our rarer monsters are,
Painted on a pole, and underwrit,
'Here may you see the tyrant."
And Sonnet's words funneled through a demon called me back
from the dusk,
and pulled my own words unmeaning from the darkness.
"I will not yield," I muttered reflexively, and his startled hands
relaxed
only for an instant.
It was enough.
I drew my breath, twisting out of his grip,
and we struggled against the whiteness of the room.
Those long hands clawing for me
as I turned him upon his back.
My blood upon him, from him, a blessing,
for the black eyes stared in wonder.
"Kill me?" he questioned through numbed lips,
as I struck him
again
and again.
"Kill me," he breathed as I had, and it was no longer a question.

But I was

I am

resigned.

"No."

I watched my execution play out.

My last surrender, if the plan should fall.

The sound of footsteps down the hall.

And my father laughed at my hesitation

through a wet mouth as red as paint.

"Why ever not," he replied, smiling up at me.

"Because," I whispered,

as the Breakers opened the door,

cocked the guns,

and smiling, lost.

"I condemn you to be you… for the rest of your life."

BLUE

Alone at the window, gazing over the crowd that had gathered,
so still and so forgotten.
What could I tell you, there, at that moment,
as you laughed at the winter sunlight,
uncaring, when I asked you why.
Descartes. Our poor tortured soul. Did he know?
What reason, Author? What purpose? You have saved nothing.
The last time I spoke to you,
I told you everything,
before they took you away with my betrayal ringing in your ears.
I gave over the correspondence to force your confession.
I directed all the Breakers with your stolen words, written
through another.
False Author, was she dead by your hand?
She was starving when I found her, and I gave her bread
for words and for her children.
Author.
Did you see the children?
Author.
Did I save you from the fire?
Did I save you?
Did I?
I never meant to hurt you.
I loved you, Author.
But you had gone too fast and too far.
I had to save Eden, no matter the cost.
You nearly stopped me at the last.
But a single life could not be worth
more than a nation.

Not even yours.
And so,
nothing could stop me.
Not even you.

They asked me, as one of those closest to her, if I wanted to see
the body after.
I didn't.
I wanted to remember her as she was.
Fearless.
Unstoppable.
Something beyond the rest of us.
But that was shattered when the bullet sounded against her head
and took the dreams of the Artists with it.
But those were dreams they no longer wanted to remember.
Something drove me down into the Palace basements where
they kept some of the bodies
that had been pulled from the wreckage of a failed rebellion.
I tried not to look at faces.
They lay side by side, like soldiers.
There, a charred child curled on its side on a stainless steel table.
Beside it a mother-shield riddled with bullets.
Author was stretched out between a man and a fallen child.
Her body was the same, only lax in death,
the delicate fingers splayed, as if reaching to the child.
But her face.
Her face.
I turned and wiped my mouth, nausea burning in my throat.
Remember. Remember. Remember.
The angels in borrowed robes.
I climbed onto the table with her under the uncaring eyes of
Breakers

who watched, one through a full mask, as if to cover scars.
And I took her into my arms
as if she was the child.
And later, when they took the body
and burnt it into ashes,
they would speak of her as the Author
as if she belonged to no-one.
And when the Camps began to rise again,
she was their Author, as if she had been always.
But no, I thought, as if I could protect her.
Not your Author.
Mine.

I watched from the window what was meant to be me.
The roar of the masses and I knew that they were calling for
Author.
But who am I?
I am finished fighting.
My face was, is, seared with the seal of Eden.
I had to go away.
After the execution, 376 was waiting to help me escape.
Why, I could not, cannot tell.
I cannot—
I cannot remember anything
but the feel of the fire.
I waited for the boy to step forward,
to tell them that I only spoke the truth.
That he was a traitor.
That he lied.
That he sent an innocent woman to torture and death,
and it was too late, too late to turn back.
To save her would have been to lose everything.
But the truth would not bring back the Artists who died
in pursuit of the Voice of Eden,
and the crowd was getting restless.
Still.
His eyes were fixed on what should have been me.
There at the failing of a revolution.
His eyes were fixed on her, on me, and I wanted him to think
that I had died.
As I would have, I will, should the plan fall.
Everything was in place,

and Galileo knew nothing.

As the aristo spoke, his pale skin gleamed in the sunlight,

and the blood has been carefully wiped away.

He shone like the birth of the world.

But I did not see it.

I saw her try to be brave for the crowd,

to put on a good show,

but her fear betrayed me.

Because the boy did not move.

And Galileo said:

"Is there anyone here who objects to this sentence?"

And I rehearsed the moment in my mind.

This was the story of the dawning of a dynasty,

and the fall of a kingdom.

This was the part where I was meant to die.

BLUE

Author is dead,
and I picked up my pen after the fall
to begin a revolution, Descartes,
that I could then, and now, begin to believe in.
I understand now.
Better that we all starve because of love than die of hate.
In our world, only genius on paper is suffered to live.
But what of the others?
There must have been a reason
that she fought so long and so hard.
Was injured, tortured, did the unthinkable,
allowing the man she loved to founder.
All for a revolution.
She stood before a crowd of people that wanted her dead.
She was willing to die, disgraced and alone,
with the people she strove to aid roaring for her blood.
For what purpose, Author?
They hated you.
And some still do,
though most call you the Martyr.
You would have given your life to save Descartes, Author.
But what of me?
Did you ever think of me?
And what of your son?
Author, you will be cursed.
Loved.
Hated.
But you will be remembered.
That was my last chance, Author,

at the end of your rebellion.
I would have saved the Camps.
I signaled to them by the death of Newton.
I fulfilled the promise I had written to the Camps under your
name.
And by the true death of Newton,
I gave them a reason to remember you as a hero.
Author
I saved you.
I saved your name.
Did I not?
I was meant to live fully under your name,
and under you, be remembered.

Newton, Galileo's lord, was dead
He spoke no more.
At last, this time, at last.
But the King lived on.
Long live the King.
We have scorched the snake,
Not killed it.
But the people began to believe in Author once more.
An Author on the side of the Artists,
not out of ideals, but out of love.
An Author that could not be neutral as—

Fire is fair.

After the Voice of Eden was dead,
they took the last books from the library
and burned them in front of the Citadel
with Newton, wrapped like a load of lumber, in a slender sheet.

The stink of him and the smoke cast into the sky.
He burned in a fire made of words.
Eden's murdered lord.
The books, they burned.
And I meant to salvage them,
and your heart from the ashes.
I destroyed them as utterly
as if I had held the match myself.
This is what you fought for?
It burned, Author.
Like you,
your work all burned to ashes.
Look at your pretty kingdom.
What is left, a few sections in the Camps?
Fire is the only thing left
that is intolerable and fair.
It burns the drivel and the masterpiece.
The hero and the villain.
You were, you are, not different.
Author, your body burnt in a fire
and you were freed from your ruined prison.
Author, I could smell the words burning
and they smelt like a revolution.
You have consumed me.
You have consumed my soul.
For fire cares for nothing,
and fire is fair.

COMET

The Martyr, the Artist, the Scientist and King.
The Martyr, the Artist, the Scientist and King.
The Martyr, the Artist, the Scientist and King.
The King is dead.
Long live the King.

Coming back to you, Darwin
is like coming home
even in the worst of circumstances.
You heard my footsteps by your chambers
echoing against the marble,
and threw open your door.
Your black eyes were near unreadable
as they always are.
But you must have been waiting.
Your dress-shirt was unbuttoned
revealing a throat as white as the marble.
But I thought of nothing.
Nothing but the fall.
I heard you call my name,
saw you, my hero, rush forward
with arms as wide as angels' wings.
And then there was nothing.
Nothing at all.

I awoke in your chambers,
propped up against your desk,
you, before me, with an aid kit,
cleaning the blood from an abrasion

that I could not remember getting.
"How are you feeling?" you inquired softly.
Darwin.
You said that you were sorry that you loved me.
"The King is dead," I murmured without sense.
"Long live the King."
And you drew back with a shuddering breath,
but your eyes seemed touched by fire.
"Long live the king," you repeated, dazed,
and shook your head in wonder.
I began to laugh, and you whipped back to alertness,
at once by my side.
"Comet—" you began,
but I stopped you, giggling hysterically—
"And long may you reign!"
Your brow creased and then understanding dawned
in your ink-black eyes.
You held me close then,
and trembled at the fate of a King.

"I have to send you to the Barracks," you whispered,
*"Only for a time. I will find a loophole. Watch for the Palace car at
Cleaning. I will find you."*
And then you shifted and grabbed my head
to gaze into my eyes with those eerie lights in yours.
*"You must do what you can. Find Blue, Comet. Let Eden burn so
that something new may grow."*
My fate, but
"How can I get him to—"
I could only think of you, at the reins of power—-
"Write him a letter."
Left and lost.

"Why me? You are the writer. I can't—"
Alone.
"Try."
And I would.
I would keep you safe.
"Don't leave me," I protested helplessly, and you smiled the
smile
that I love and remembered.
"I will never leave you, Scientist."
"I need you."
And as footsteps sounded,
the cock of the rifles
to escort me.
You held me, then, Darwin.
For a very long time.

BREAKER 256

Why did I do it?
Had the people thought that I lived,
I am sure that would have been the question
that I would have been asked.
But then again, had they known I lived,
I would not have lived much longer.
The last time I saw the outside,
before my time sequestered,
they hated me.
They hated me, and wanted me dead.
For in their minds, I had lied to them.
I had led them to the slaughter,
had dangled Newton as a prize above their heads
only to have their sons, their daughters,
shot down in a hail of gunfire and then burned.
But it was not me!
Only the Artist, working through an innocent.
You see, I am innocent!
But I am not.
I am not.
Why did I do it?
I know my answer, forever repeated,
so much that it has become meaningless.
Because it is better to die by overpopulation
Then survive artificially in a system of hate.
But perhaps it was simpler than that.
Perhaps it was simply that I was one of them.
That I had always considered myself a traitor
when I had joined the State as a Breaker.

Blue never understood.
But I had been so certain.
I had thought that I had seen men hungry.
I had thought that I had seen enough horrors
to damn the entire human race
without a guilty twinge for my principles.
Freedom rather than repression.
Hope rather than fear.
This I still believe.
But was the cause worth the cost?
Can one ever be sure?

COMET

I was once a child.
Of what fragility is a motivation?
I should have been on the side of the rebellion.
Darwin and I are on neither side but Darwin tells me—
the Martyr was the champion of the revolution
before she faded away.
And the Artist was on the side of the State,
before he thought the Martyr dead.
And what are we? Using the cause of the Artists
to further a new rebellion.
I dress for the Barracks,
and hidden with me are the pages of the Edicts
to give to the Artist.
Paper is precious, and he shall write a new civilization
on the back of the old.
Bound in the metal pieces torn from a booklet
once owned by a boy with laughing dark eyes and dark hair.
56859.
My friend was killed in the Hives after he failed his CEE.
My friend gave me his book of Edicts to keep me safe,
and this is all that is left of him.
One inch.
But it is enough.
Enough for the boy that did not survive long enough to get a
name.
Enough for the boy that is forgotten already.
This system will be stripped of its power.
There will, must be a better way.
But first, the glorious revolution.

And then the take over, the take over that must be viewed as a
betrayal.
Let this revolution be written on the pages
torn from the book of the Edicts.
Let Author reign once more,
but to our purposes.
Let it begin,
and let the world burn if only to save a remnant.
For one day, the State will say,
we will be dead.
But not today.
We are not dead today.

CONFLAGRATION

BLUE

The time of the Cull
They say that it starts out
with a tickle at the back of the throat
and reddish eyes,
a feverish brow and aching limbs.
Then comes the swellings all over the body and fatigue.
Your whole body feels like it is burning
and your hair and teeth begin to fall out as the lesions grow.
I have seen men that should have long been dead.
And I write to stave off forgetting.
Cleaning Day has moved to all days
but my writing has not hastened.
Still a letter once a month from the stranger
this time to tell me to continue for
the draft is not complete.
To rally the soldiers once more.
The traitors and the empty men.
But I have seen men that should have been dead.
Men with eyes as blank as gray stones.
Men that cannot stand
and so were pulled to the side and shot like horses.
And the Cleaners move their sticks in decisiveness
and nod their bird-like masks like strange flowers.
Masks or faces?

I start at a cough and will wait
until the sickness overtakes my own body.
I cannot hurry my work for
inspiration keeps eluding me.
But I cannot die, not yet.
I have felt the burning in my throat,
and yesterday, a lesion
like the mark of a whore upon my hand.
But I will try to remember
until the day that I am dead.
They have stopped shooting men
as that leaves a corpse,
and they have taking to burning.
I will try.
I will try.
I will try to remember.

THE SCIENTIST

To the Artist:
Ah yes, how you hate that name!
How you thought yourself better!
But this is my last letter.
Our last letter.
For who then wrote to the people
in the space that you were gone in the Barracks,
and my imprisonment?
Your final product must be perfect,
and after you pass it down the line
it will be in the Camps tonight.
I never lied to you, Artist.
I never said that you had a chance.
We both know that you didn't.
That was why you agreed to write this for me.
The last desperate errand for atonement.
For your Author.
This is the end, Blue.
You are going to die.
You have probably reached a settled conclusion about this
and feel yourself to be a martyr.
You may think to yourself,
that it is better to die a gallant death
than to be taken out and shot like a dog

in a crowded kennel.
Or burned like a piece of rubbish
meant to be thrown away.
But death is not dramatic, Artist, and death is not remembered.
Death is not where you go
to meet the angels.
The angels are here,
and they wish that they were human.
Listen to me.
I will leave you nothing.
Not even your life.
Not even your lie.
For death is not the glory of redemption.
It is sweat, and shit, and blood.
You will not be redeemed by bullets or flame.
You will not be redeemed by love.
Once you had loved,
and apologized to no one.
I wish that I had known you then.
But, no matter.
For you were always owed a fall, my Artist.
Did you enjoy the trip?

—The Scientist

PART SIX: BARREN

EDICT 9095: A new edict has been formed. The prerogative of the State is the safety of its citizenry. There shall be no more choosing to take on the duty of the Breakers. All those who score across all areas of the CEE shall see joining the Breakers mandatory. If a man is a Breaker, that man belongs to the State. If a review proves that an offender is culpable of severing this covenant, that man will be imprisoned or else put to death.

BREAKER 256

376
and the escape.
I was to be placed in the Barracks.
A heavy hand held mine
that had blood under the fingernails.

Everything was ready for the Barracks.
But first, the Camps and home.
Poet's Camp as we arrived was near deserted.
Shanty town, slow burn of fires,
the cast of the trash, and starving dogs.
But the boy confessed False Author's name,
and that she had had children.
The tilted shack
that the leader Dante had once called throne
was waiting.
So 376 held my hand tightly
But why did the dog betray his master?
and we went inside.
The forgotten infant was there,
screaming in a makeshift crib,
and there was a boy with a dirty face,
who sat on the floor and played.
My heart went out to him
in one terrible instant
as I stepped forward into the light,
removed my mask to clear my sight.

And at the sight of my ruined face
the boy began to scream.
"No," I whispered, as my eyes burned.
"No, I will protect you."
And I reached out my hand.
376 was there for him in an instant, ripping off his mask
to reveal himself as human.
Just as I revealed myself as monster.
And the boy clung to the big man, burying his face in his chest.
No time for reflection, the other, the infant,
crying angrily, and far too thin.
Its furious cries and the sobs of the boy filled the shack.
I held it close to my breast and glanced at 376,
who gently put aside the child and went to my side.
We must take them both to the nearest Hive, first, he whispered.
But I shook my head.
"The Hives are not safe."
The Citadel will once more aid the Camps.
The rebellion will soon be ended.
They all think you dead,
376 replied, softly, reasonably,
and his eyes were serene and far away.
It is the only way.
The boy, without hearing, regained his feet,
wiping at his eyes with the back of his hand
and asked: "Where is my mother?"
And 376 answered:
Your mother is dead.

COMET

And so to us angels aspire.
One died for treason
The other for fire?

Time before the Barracks.
Darwin, you warned me
that you would not be with me
when the time came.
That last time,
before they took me away,
you tried to keep me safe.
"The time of the Cull has already begun,"
you murmured,
"The time of sickness that the Cleaners have released in
the Barracks.
I will protect you,
but only the strong will survive."
And then you held me at arm's length,
gazing fiercely into my eyes.
"Eat, and stay strong. The Cleaners are under my command
now that my father is dead.
But who they choose is not under my command.
Stay safe, and find the Artist."
The Artist. Find him.
Artist.
Barracks.
Cleaners.
Words from a nightmare,
tales told to frighten children,

little boys swapping stories
at night-time in the Hives.
I remember the Cleaners.
There are some who say that
their heads are like the heads of birds,
elongated and strange,
and that their robes are white.
They only start their selection at the command
of the Human Services Coordinator.
"You are their commander?" I questioned,
and you smiled and nodded.
Their heads are smooth and white
like the skulls of the angels,
but their skins over bones—
"Some say," I murmured, "that their masks are
pieced together from the bleached skins of liars."
And you at long last—
you looked away.
"The Breakers wear masks,"
You replied softly.
"What the Cleaners have,
are not masks.
merely faces."
And I shook away the image
of a scabrous skin, and said:
"So what are they then? Masks or faces?"
And you smiled
your manufactured little smile
and said:
"Sometimes what were masks
turn into faces."
And the sweetness of your confession

that you loved me as
one loves something that
one is fond of.
And as you lifted your head
to hear the sound of leaden boots
meant to bring me away,
you embraced me,
and I jumped as I felt
the needle meant to save me.
For you showed the syringe
with all of it empty.
And your eyes—
they were empty.
When the Breakers came, and
they took me away.

FADE

BLUE

I dreamed of a man in a fire.
He was with the sickness.
And the masks of the Cleaners
were not masks at all but faces.
They dragged him to the makeshift fire
and he screamed as they tied him to a pyre of rubbish.
And he screamed as they lit the match.
But he was sick
and fire purifies all things.
Fire is fair.
And my letter
to the last
has been given to the assumed Descartes.
The one that calls himself Scientist
and will be in the Camps tonight.
I have seen men roasting on our merry fires.
They now burn them in the Barracks
to keep the Breakers and Cleaners from infection.
But they do not bother to kill them first.
And in my dream,
the man sang to me as his hair caught on fire
and the light was a crescendo.
He sang that all men,
that all men deserve a fall.

To be a constellation of stars
in a riot of blood.
And here I am.
I will twist the metal clasp
from each of the letters.
And I will walk to the fire,
when all the Barracks burn.

BREAKER 256

---

376 has used his influence as Eden's best Breaker
to guarantee me employment.
I am to stay here in the Barracks for the rest of my days
until he is found out.
Or civilization crumbles.

Whichever comes first.

The tall dark figure in an industrial mask.
He cleaned my facial burns with a cloth and alcohol from a
stolen kit
and his eyes behind the mask were dark and steady.
"Our fallen hero."
I winced away from his touch and he soothed me,
waiting for a moment until I could take the healing.
"Why do you call me this?"
He paused, turning my head back.
All business.
And then said:
"Is that not what you are? You cannot be a martyr."
The tiny room was stifling and the sweat had begun to run into
his eyes.
He carefully snapped off his mask and added casually—

"You have to be dead to qualify."

"I led an innocent to her death, 376," I whispered and my words were loud in the small room

as if I had shouted my confession.

The cloth ghosted over my useless eye and I bit my lip.

I would not cry out.

Not here, not now.

376 watched me, the slender face pale, the eyes under arched by exhaustion.

"You did what you had to do," he replied finally.

"Why help me now?" I retorted into his startled face.

"You near killed me. You were against me."

Memories.

His fractured form above my sight in a darkened room.

Descartes.

"You could kill me now. There is still time. If they find out you saved me—"

And he hesitated, shaking his head.

"I am the leader of the revolution, I am—"

"But you are not now, 256. You are nothing again once more."

The guileless eyes were troubled.

"Why did you torture me," I murmured.

"Why didn't you stop then? Why did you not save my brother and Descartes?

Why did you kill innocents—"

"And you did not?"

There was no venom in his mild reply. He had simply asked a question.

"The child under my care…my daughter, is dead," he answered quietly.

"Galileo had held her for years, held her life over my head in the Hives.

She was killed after my questioning of Descartes.
Your lover would not speak so I had him write. He only wrote a word.
He would not betray you."
And the cloth was folded and put away.
"What did he write you?"
"Write."
"Now I could take a risk, I can choose my way. I chose to save you, but to retain my Duty."
"But the Duty is wrong! You do not even have a cause—nothing to fight for."
"If I stop now, I will be apprehended. You will be found out, condemned.
While I serve with my men, you live."
"Then kill me."
And he looked at me with unspeakably weary eyes.
"While I serve," he answered softly, *"Your son still has a chance of protection.*
For once, think of him."
And something in me trusted, trusts, him.
This honest man, too fair to lie.
Did you so often protect children?
The child-made bracelet had been put away.
I nodded and he placed a hand on my shoulder.
"Hive 45834," I whispered. "Keep my son alive… as long as you can."
"As long as I can, and I will add him to the fold," he replied,
and a genuine smile touched his lips.
There and gone so quickly I could scarcely believe in its existence.
"Good, Author," he whispered,
and my head lifted at the sound of what has become my name.

It would be the last time that I would hear it
and have it meant for me.
"Now you *have nothing left to lose."*

For who is it to say
that the warden is not the prisoner?

COMET

Your era was over, wasn't it?
Your time, it was close to over.
Now then, a chance to set things right.
How could he had ever thought that you were the cause of my
letters?
My silent roommate.
We were placed together by design.
Look at you.

Descartes would not eat in the Barracks.
He did not speak.
He lay staring at the ceiling as if to find images written in stone
or faced the wall.
He did not talk of suffering,
but sometimes in the night,
I would hear savagely stifled cries in the darkness
and other times nothing.
Only strange eyes red-rimmed
gazing as if to find a window.
Was he ill? Dying?
I am safe for now. Darwin's medicine will last as long as it may—
Descartes.
The wound, was it from a stunner?
It must had healed many years ago.
But you still wore a bandage as a reminder.
Didn't you?
Descartes.
Flesh of my flesh and blood of my blood.
Your son, the foolish Artist, the betrayer of the Camps, he lives.

He lives.

Look at me.

But he looked at no one.

When I would take the pointed straw, and turn it to my wrist,

to write in human ink,

with all my little tricks,

he shuddered,

and murmured: *"Write."*

Was that the last word that anyone said to you?

You could not speak another.

It stood for hatred, fear, cajoling, confusion, all.

The last word before the fall.

When I write, it is under your name.

For you cannot write anymore, Aristo-who-writes.

No matter.

You were content to remember your Author

and I must protect what is mine.

BLUE

Think for the children.
Remember the words that live on.
And wait for the signal that burns.

There will be a bonfire tonight,
but I do not think I will live to see it.
They must have caught on to our letters.
Assumed Descartes,
Uncertain scribbler.
The boys who killed the angels.
And even if the execution failed,
I would not pass the Cleaning.
I am sick,
I am smiling.
I do not sleep.
I only write to stave off forgetting,
and my kingdom is traced behind my eyelids
as if fired behind by the sun.
You promised me, nothing, really, false writer.
Only to take part in the leveling of a kingdom.
Young Darwin is crowned and the King is dead
by the precise hand of a Scientist.
False writer—
soon I will be dead.

And the fair Author,
that lives inside my head
will die with me.
I fold up my letter,
written within the margins of the Edicts, and smile.
"Remember me," I say,
even though, Scientist,
we both know it to be nothing.
Remember the one that was no longer an Artist,
for once I had apologized to no one
and once I had loved.

TO THE CAMPS: THE SCIENTIST

AUTHOR

Do be patient. Wait, remember me
And think for the light.
Remember for the words, free
Will be the signal that in night
In our children, that live. For the tree
Nearer here burns on ever bright.

COMET

I remember the day that Descartes died.
During Cleaning, the cells had stood open,
and someone shot his complicated brains out into the snow.
No one knew who did it,
but we all knew the reason,
for no one save myself and the traitor
knew the aristo-who-wrote.
That day, I had passed Cleaning,
and my first letter down the line,
to linger in the hands of the Artist.
And when I returned
the woman had found him before any of us.
We found Descartes.
He is dead.
They put a bullet
through his head.
The woman who cleaned the cells,
the woman with the hidden face,
she held him in the center of our cell
and she held him like a child.
The aristo-who-wrote,
who had risked everything,
would never write again.

Descartes.
You lay in her arms
as if you were sleeping.
As perfect as a fallen angel.
Your face as pure as marble,
the side destroyed away.
The stink of him and the thought of a fire.
Did they tell her that you were dead back in the Palaces?
It must have been Author.
For I knew it then.
The tears, even stranger as she held you,
were almost your tears.
"Fly for the both of us."
And she bent to kiss you.
Her lips were white by fire, Descartes,
and she must have loved you.

But now, no more.
A riot in the Barracks,
for they heard of the Camps' uprising.
The prisoners were out of their cages.
It's Cleaning Day, It's Cleaning Day.
And the Artist—Blue was there, I could feel him.
Does art need to be beautiful?
Does love need to be fair?
It is your grotesqueness that I find beautiful.
Artist.
You kept every one of my letters,
and with your inventive mind
saved each metal clasp
to twist into the tree of Eden.
The blaze in the parade grounds

was it the forge of your soul,
or your funerary pyre?
And the look on your face was transported,
beyond the veil of pain or pity.
The serene countenance of
a demon or an angel.
Your makeshift brand cast away,
and you lifted your arms in front of the flame
and screamed wordlessly into the sky.
My Artist.
Your Author is dead to the potential of the world.
What she is now can do nothing.
But oh, the weeping sore of a pointless sacrifice!
For you thought to be like her!
"I am like you."
And you crumpled to your knees
as the Breakers rushed to put out the flame,
to put out your heart for
"I am like you."

*For fire cares for nothing
and fire is fair.*

I watched the Artist's pitiful figure
recoil in his cell from the light
that emitted past the door like an accusatory finger.
He was shrunken, bloodied from the sickness.
His toothless mouth caved in.
His hair all gone.
He scrabbled to stay out of my searching.
His face that caught the light

like a gleam of trout in a stream,
was tight and shiny where the brand had burned
the mark of Eden into his unwashed skin.
He had branded himself a traitor to mark himself a hero.
His right eye was gone, shrunk in its socket,
the other eye peering, peering.
Poor parody of a tragedy, Blue.
A mockery of what should have happened to your Author.
What a story that would have been!
The spurned hero's death by firing-squad.
How anticlimactic, what she is now.
The woman without a face
and the woman without a name,
whose hand trembles as she sweeps the filth away
from a forgotten life.
And I was like my Artist,
with all morality stripped away.
An apex predator straining to the light.
A mythical tiger with its muzzle up to the eyes
in the blood of its living prey.
And I stood, in my imagined shining
over the trembling wreckage of a perfect tragedy.
For you gazed up at me in supplication,
with that one bright eye shining,
and in cruelty I told you that
"Author lives."
And in duality I told you
"Your mother lives."
Perfect whore, 256!
No time in a rebellion to know your own son.
Author waited for you to start the rebellion, Blue.
Twelve years, she waited to start the rebellion.

And when I was born of your unnatural union,
she did not spare a thought for me.
I am you as surely as I am Descartes remade.
Blue, I am you had you learned to love.
Blue, I am you if you could not remember.
I am you if you were reborn.
The final triumph of logic over emotion.
But everything I did, Artist, I did it for love.
You never loved your Author.
Had you loved her,
you would have allowed the State to crumble to fall into ruins
and you would have danced upon the pieces.
I would allow every man, woman, and child to die
if only my love would live.
But he lives and all is well.
Together we shall save the State.
And the world had no place for you.
I watched you that day burn with a shame
that was deeper than any agony
you could inflict upon yourself.
"Who?" you murmured,
and I told you who she was.
Who I am.
And I looked to my letters and smiled.
"The Scientist and your son," I replied.
"The writer and your muse."
"But I am a savior from hell," I reminded.
"And you are not to trust me."

BREAKER 256

Au clair de la lune,
On n'y voit qu'un peu.
On chercha la plume,
On chercha le feu.
En cherchant d'la sorte,
Je n'sais c'qu'on trouva;
Mais je sais qu'la porte
Sur eux se ferma.

Every inch of me is dead.
Save for one.
One inch.
Blue.
What were you thinking, to fall in love with me?
And it was love, wasn't it, in the beginning?
I closed my eyes to it, and called you liar,
your betrayal merely confirming what I already had suspected.
But no, you loved me.
Or rather, you loved the mask, the false face, the creation
in your own poisoned mind, of what I was meant to be.
What will they write of me?
Will I be their hero, as I was yours?
Until I rebelled only to reveal my fragility.
My frailty.
For I was human, I had tempests, and moments of weakness
and I was frightened of what lay ahead.
More frightened than I can tell you.
Once my heart burned with the fires of revolution.

But they are gone, now.
Faded away.
There is nothing to be frightened of any longer.
My eyes burn and my hands are shaking.
Sometimes, I will hear something from the outside,
376 is old, and soon will face the firing squad,
sentenced by his age.
But still, he tells me of the world and
something about the Scientist
and how the Camps were to be freed
as Galileo was slaughtered.
My heart at this would burn once more,
but it was the feeble flickering of near-dead coals
that, when the promise was not fulfilled died just as quickly.
Do you remember the day that they first brought you in?
In here to the Barracks for ending the life of Newton?
How you fought them?
How you cursed and spat at their feet?
I cannot look at you now.
They say that you have the sickness from the Cull,
but that the letter, the last letter
that your Scientist will distribute
will be in the Camps tonight.
And that the world will be consumed utterly.
Purified by destruction,
the face of chaos to pave way for freedom.
The opposite of your dream.
For you never believed my ideals.
You took up the pen because you loved me,
because your guilt ate at and corroded your heart.
Because the last shred of humanity in you demands to be
acknowledged and justified.

Your beloved State will crumble.
But to what end?
What has the Scientist planned?
376 knows nothing of that, so neither do I.
You never should have loved me, Blue.
Perhaps I should have loved you.
And I do, enough to keep you from the burning,
that your sickness would set you for a fate.
They were going to burn you alive and rake the ashes.
But I had a word with the one man
whose influence still prevails.
376 is old, and soon they will take him out
behind the sheds, like an old horse that has worked too long and
too hard.
But with his influence,
I give you my last gift.
You will die at the barrel of a gun,
with your flesh seared with the mark of a traitor
and a lie coiled into the chambers of your heart.

COMET

The words that died in the cold and in the snow.
And do not shoot the messenger.
I was with Breakers when Blue died, in the cell,
surrounded by my letters.
The Artist laughed at the failing of a revolution with a wild dark
humor,
as if he could not believe that he had gone so far, and fought so
well,
only to die there at the last.
He was still laughing when they turned the guns on him.
How many bullets does it take to extinguish a soul as great as
that of a traitor?
He never forgave himself, and it took too many.
I watched my father and my brother die.
I could not think, I could not feel.
When the Breakers were satisfied, my old 376 turned them to
go.
I could not save him, nor do any more damage.
So I faced the dying man
with the self-brand of the Martyr
whose letter had burned so near my heart.
The revolution would have soon begun,
but first I would slip in the blood of the Artist.
Where was Darwin? Why hadn't he come?
Blue was leaning against the wall, cradling his body with both
hands
as if to keep in his heart.
The old woman who cleaned the cells stood at the door,
and when he called, she came to him.

I had never seen her face,
but I knew she must be beautiful.
He reached up.
His hand tugged as if to keep himself from falling,
and the hood fell away.
From where I was standing, I could not see her face.
I only saw the expression on his,
before he fell away.
The information passed, and footsteps down the hall.
She looked down at the dead man, turned, and said
"Remember,"
in a voice like a violin gathering up all the sadness in the world.
And in the instant before I left, upon her I could see
the tracing of a tree's branches burnt.
So many, many fires ago.

BREAKER 256

I watched you from the door
as the Breakers came in
with their gleaming uniforms.
And my old friend, 376, hounder and savior,
leading them, head held high,
like an old horse proud to once more be set in the traces.
The only thing left for 376 now, was myself and the Duty.
He hated the State, but could not bring himself to betray
once more.
And you knew of your death, Blue, you were ready.
Your letter was in the Camps.
We are a matched set, are we not, by your making?
I watched you as you struggled.
You died hard Blue,
not with a sigh, but with a struggle,
choking and retching,
scrabbling for the light.
You are nothing that I remember.
The boy who loved me had been beautiful.
Insolently beautiful.
But your face and body were ravaged from the sickness,
rendered hardly human by the scarring of your makeshift brand.
A mockery of my own suffering.
The mark of Eden to skin is the seal of a traitor.
And that you were, as surely as I was, enemy to the State.
But you and I—
You and I.
Can we be called the same?
Memories of you in the dark,

your compact body against mine.
Your idiot whispering of love and devotion.
Your beaming of pride, your rages, and your jealousies.
Your betrayal.
I give you my last gift after execution.
Me.
My face revealed, your hand lingered upon my cheek
covering the ruined side of my face.
You made me my mask,
revealing me to be a creature once again of innocence.
I wish I could have loved you.
But for your last seconds, I will be who you wished me to be.
In your dying eyes, my age would fall away.
I would be beautiful once more.
Your eyes met mine, Blue,
and for an instant, I saw the worshipful boy,
the foolish boy that loved me.
And I saw that he was sorry.
For I am like you.
And then something in your good eye dimmed
and I watched you fall away.

COMET

What could I do?
The riot.
I waited
as insidiously, relentlessly
the snow began to fall
upon the living and the dead,
in the prison blocks, the parade ground,
and behind the sheds,
where men were once shot like horses
and a tangle of figures lay frozen on the ground.

The warden and the prisoner.

So quickly.
He must have seen the insurgent,
chased him,
brought him down in the snow—

The prisoner, emaciated, his face hidden by his hair
lay dead, his fist still clenched loosely to the rifle
whose barrel was resting against the chest of his enemy.
His enemy who was still alive.
Who was still alert as I approached,
but did not call out, did not say a thing,
only rested his cheek against the snow,
and waited to die.

As I waited.

It was too late for him.

376.

The great dark eyes were clouding.
But even there, in his dying,
there was still a glory to him,
a simplistic grandeur
that altered the plain black uniform.
Gone was his strength and his standing.
The hair that was once sable was now streaked with silver.
But the eyes —
the eyes were always the same.
And it was, it is, just a job, those steady eyes revealed
as Eden's best Breaker tore his gaze from mine
to look to the prisoner that he had apprehended,
before he fell away.

Now he lies forever linked in chase.
The prisoner and the warden.
The errant knight and knave.
As it should and rightfully be
under that shared canopy
of dead and dying stars.

No pleasure in the chase.
No pain in the fall.

BREAKER 256

The words that died in the cold and the snow.
But did they die?
Did they ever live?
That is the real question.
To what end is all striving?
To what purpose?
What then, is the right?

"Write."

Now Descartes is finally dead.
They put a bullet through his head.

Quickly, now.
What is the unalterable truth, the unquestionable morality?
I thought that I knew.
And it was in a single moment, a second of realizing that I
would do anything it took
to further the cause, to further our goal,
that I understood that we were not so different.
The Martyr.
The Scientist.
The Artist.
Each just a player in a game so beyond us,
we could not grasp the margins or consequences.
But I understand.
I understand now.
Now that the flames for me have died away
and my hands shake too much

to further a revolution.
No matter.
The books are gone.
But somewhere in the Camps,
Live on the words.
And words know how to wait.
The one who may be a savior,
The Scientist,
is the one who slew an angel.
And the tree of knowledge burns brightly in the Citadel.
I can see the flames from the window of my small quarters,
sequestered in the Barracks.
It burns, and the ashes raked from it
will be as bright as the branches.

COMET

The back of the Palace car.
And I had come home to you, Darwin.
But such a contrast we made!
I was bruised and covered
in the blood of the Artist,
and you were, as always, impeccably poised,
a statue of marble in a three-piece suit.
Perfect but for a tiny dot of blood that had spotted your lapel.
I doubt you noticed it, you were too concerned for me.
My body was wracked with coughs,
and you soothed me, offering me medicine.
It had been close. You had tried to protect me.
But it had been done—
"The Artist is dead," I whispered.
"I know. Your time in the Barracks is over."
And you turned your head away.
"I had stated that I had coerced you to the Citadel."
"Testified that I had ordered
The death of Galileo.
They will not overrule me."
And the faintest of smiles touched the edge of your lips
as immaterial as breath off a blade.
"Scientist, you are free."

But where were you, Darwin?
Where were you after the Artist died?
I stood shivering in the Barracks for far too long.
376 is dead.
But perhaps I heard

279

a single disjointed gunshot in the break.
Perhaps.
Darwin.
"You found Author, as I did," I murmured.
"Breaker 256," you corrected, without bothering to think.
"Then you know I cannot be free," I replied softly.
"Not while she lives. While she lives, the old rebellion stays to smother the new."
And you looked at me then, your eyes old and immeasurably weary.
I felt as though I lingered upon the edge of the abyss, held up only by a dying star
that might collapse at any moment, to send me spiraling down into the darkness.
And I understood then.
I understood the spot upon the lapel
and the lingering gunshot on the frosty air
that I swore might have been just
another sound in the cacophony.
What was it you told me that your father told her?
I condemn you to be you, as long as you live.
As long as you—

And does she live, Darwin?
Or did the new revolution murder the old in understanding?
Were you merciful, is her nightmare over?
You will not tell me.
But it does not matter, does it?
Breaker 256 is finished.
Only Author lives on.

For it is the words

That defines immortality.
It is the mere fact
That the words exist at all.

And this I believe.

I reached forward to your lax hand
that rested on the seat between us,
and at first, you jerked away
as if touched by fire.
And I watched your inexpressible composure shatter slowly,
as the cracks in your disguise began to show.
All the hideousness of humanity,
the pettiness, the hurt, the anger,
and a thousand transient emotions
warring for space upon the planes of your face.
My hideous darling and my monster love.
What a pair we were, we are.
For I am like you.
The human who thought he was an angel.
And
the angel who thought it was human.
And I am like you.
I looked at your face, that I know better than my own.
What strange thoughts capered beyond that ridge of bone?
I reached for your hand and this time
you did not pull away
and we sat without a word.
We will change everything.
Darwin, we shall change the history books,
as you believed so many years ago.
You were yourself again.

And your black eyes did not flicker,
did not register a thing.
But you trembled, Darwin,
at the duty of a King.

AUTHOR

Do be *patient*. **Wait,** *remember* me
And *think* **for** *the* light.
Remember *for* **the** *words,* free
Will be *the* **signal** *that* in night
In our *children,* **that** *live.* For the tree
Nearer here **burns** *on* ever bright.

We did what we thought was right.

PART SEVEN: PLANTING

COMET

Who's son am I?
The Citadel is on fire,
and children starve in the streets.
Far off, far off, the gunshots sound.
And our Human Services Coordinator Darwin sits at his desk
in a state of eerie calm,
and watches the conflagration with mournful eyes over tented
fingers.
"Take this to the Camps. Quickly."
Darwin nods at me in the darkness, and flourishes the name
Author at the top of the page.
I turn to go with the message when he calls me back.
"And Comet?"
*"I grow young and you grow old. How long will we have, do you
think?"*
I pause to stave off forgetting and answer—
"Long enough for Eden?"
For I stand there, shivering with fever, with the new world order
in my hand
and the smile he gives me could stop a revolution.
"Yes."
"For I grow downwards, like a turnip," he whispers as the
treacherous pen begins again to write.
"But never fear, for my roots are strong and deep."

EPILOGUE

Ex igne veritas

This world
ever was,
and is,
and shall be,
ever-living fire,
in measures being kindled
and
in measure going out.

A LIST OF MAJOR EVENTS

The Early Years

The Censor occurs. The State of Eden is created.

The State is separated into Palaces and Camps.

The Edicts are written and formulated.

GALILEO and NEWTON, the Voice of Eden, are created.

DESCARTES is created.

BREAKER 256 is born.

BREAKER 376 is born.

DARWIN is created.

BREAKER 256 tests into the Breakers.

The beginning of the first Author: BREAKER 256

BREAKER 256 becomes radicalized.

BREAKER 256 meets DESCARTES.

BREAKER 256 and DESCARTES enter into a relationship and plan the first revolution.

DESCARTES and BREAKER 256 have a child.

BLUE is born.

Twelve years after their child is born, DESCARTES and BREAKER 256 begin the first revolution. BREAKER 256 releases information to the Camps under the pen name of AUTHOR.

The decline of the first Author: BREAKER 256

BLUE tests into working for the Palaces and begins work for the State.

Four years later, BLUE meets BREAKER 256.

BREAKER 256 and BLUE begin a relationship.

GALILEO asks BLUE to find out if BREAKER 256 is the one releasing information to the Camps under the name of AUTHOR.

BREAKER 256 creates a plan to silence NEWTON, the Voice of Eden.

BREAKER 256 and BLUE have a child.

COMET is born.

BLUE goes into Poet's Camp and hires POESY, the widow of DANTE, to compose a false message to the Camps under the same pen name that BREAKER 256 uses, AUTHOR, to drive the people of the Camps into a trap.

BLUE convinces BREAKER 256 that POESY or "False Author" was the one who set the trap.

BLUE gives over the correspondence between DESCARTES and BREAKER 256 marking her as the true AUTHOR.

BREAKER 256 and BREAKER 376 create a plan to punish POESY/ "False Author" and to protect BREAKER 256.

GALILEO reveals that BREAKER 256 is AUTHOR, and has her branded with the mark of Eden as a traitor. BREAKER 256 is sentenced to death.

DESCARTES is sent to the Barracks.

BREAKER 376 helps BREAKER 256 escape. POESY/ "False Author" is executed publicly in BREAKER 256's place, causing most people, including BLUE, to believe BREAKER 256 and therefore AUTHOR, is dead. BLUE switches to the side of the rebellion.

BREAKER 376 gains BREAKER 256 employment in disguise in the Barracks.

The beginning and decline of the second Author: BLUE

BLUE decides to redeem BREAKER 256 by killing NEWTON, the Voice of Eden.

GALILEO takes over as the Voice of Eden.

BLUE is captured, and is sent to the Barracks.

The arc of the Scientist: COMET

COMET tests into the Palaces to begin work as a scientist.

DARWIN reveals to COMET the inequalities in life expectancies between Palaces and Camps.

COMET becomes radicalized.

DARWIN begins and ends a project with COMET to attempt to rectify the inequalities in life expectancies between Palaces and Camps.

DARWIN releases information about the project to the Camps.

A deadly virus ("The Cull") is released in the Barracks to curb the prison population.

DARWIN and COMET plan to kill GALILEO.

COMET kills GALILEO.

DARWIN takes over as Human Services Coordinator in GALILEO's place.

DARWIN has COMET arrested and sent to the Barracks to find BLUE and to convince him to create one last message under the pen name AUTHOR for the Camps.

The Joining of the Story-lines

COMET meets DESCARTES in the Barracks.

DESCARTES is killed by another prisoner. COMET comes into contact with BREAKER 256.

COMET contacts BLUE by writing to him under the name of DESCARTES and sending the letter to him during the prison inspection, attempting to convince him to write the message to the Camps.

COMET and BLUE remain in correspondence with each other, crafting the draft that will get sent to the Camps.

COMET reveals his true identity to BLUE in his last letter.

COMET and BLUE meet, and BLUE hands over the letter that is meant for the Camps.

BLUE comes into contact with BREAKER 256 and is killed.

BREAKER 376 is killed. BREAKER 256 is presumed to be killed.

COMET is rescued by DARWIN from the Barracks and taken back to the Palaces.

BLUE's final letter is sent to the Camps.

DARWIN writes a message to the Camps under the pen name of AUTHOR to spur on the revolution, hoping to build a new State upon what is left after the revolution.

About the Author

G.L. Adamson is a mysterious and shadowy figure who enjoys writing things down. Adamson has a wide range of works, ranging from horror and suspense fiction, to sci-fi, to urban fantasy and conservation literature. Her debut novel with Greyhart Press, "The Death of the Wave", is a dystopian fantasy novel set in an oppressive state that satirizes standardized testing.

When she isn't writing books, she studies wildlife management and nonprofit management at a university, interviews Maasai pastoralists about wildlife conflict, hikes strange mountains, saves murderous owls, creates plays and screenplays and builds tiny scaled models of medieval siege weaponry.

About The Death of the Wave

A villain always thinks himself the hero. That is the main point that drove this book, as it is told through three distinct points of view around several fictional historical events, each looking at the events from a different side. There's several rebellions in this novel, all revolving around a character that seems to be the main protagonist, but the point of the book is that there is a tendency to think that one is in the right.

What I hoped this book to challenge, apart from ideas such as standardized testing, educational systems, wealth distribution, career biases towards the arts and the sciences and censorship, is the idea that it is harder than one things to qualify a 'heroic' character. There are many characters in this novel. Some do extraordinary things. All do some pretty awful things in order to further their cause, and every last one thinks that they are the hero of their own story, and in that way, they are right.

I was working on this story when I was in London and Dublin in the summer of 2012, scribbling on odds and ends of paper and spending far too much time in the hotel lobby, drinking coffee and typing until 3AM in the morning, and a lot of the story was done in a straight shot, written without stopping and without many blocks. I had seen *Les Miserables* in West End a week earlier and had been struck by the intensity of the idea of a multi-character plot centered around a rebellion, but I wanted to clearly deconstruct the idea in my own work that the freedom fighters are always intrinsically the ones in the right. Another major influence on this work was Alan Moore's *V for Vendetta,* in the idea of a freedom fighter that commits horrible acts in the quest for justice.

The title itself was influenced by a line in Hunter S. Thompson's *Fear and Loathing in Las Vegas,* that described the decade of the sixties as a wave that 'climbed higher and higher, and then finally broke and rolled back' and I think that that kind of imagery was appropriate for the title of this work. The rebellions and events are like a series of waves that seem unending and invincible, only to crash in the end, petering out with ripples that echo in influence once the main event had concluded.

In general for this work, I was influenced a great deal by such authors such as George R.R. Martin, who also is known for works that deconstruct the idea of a singular protagonist or objective morality, as well as the obvious influences of Aldous Huxley, George Orwell, and Ray Bradbury. The existential philosopher Sartre was a major influence on the novel as well. This work is considered to be a piece of dystopian fiction, and I made the choice to write it in unrhymed verse as that seemed to reflect the stark and desolate mood of the piece better than prose. All of these influences tied together and found a place in the *Death of the Wave.*

- G. L. Adamson, December 2013

About Greyhart Press

Talk to us on Twitter (@GreyhartPress)
or email (editors@greyhartpress.com)

Greyhart Press

Greyhart Press is an indie publisher of quality genre fiction: fantasy, science fiction, horror, and some stories that defy description.

We publish eBooks and print-on-demand paperbacks through online retailers. That's great for us and for you, because we don't have to worry about all that costly hassle of stock-holding and distribution. Instead we can concentrate on finding great stories AND giving some away for free!

Visit our free story promotion page today for no-strings-attached free downloads.

Would you like to read our eBooks for free?

If so, our READ… REVIEW… REPEAT… promotion is for you.

See our website for more details.
www.greyhartpress.com